# The Most Awfullest Crime of the Year:

## Gawd Almighty and The Corn

## A Massanutten Tale

# An Artzy Chicks Mystery

**by**

**Judith Lucci**

**An Artzy Chicks Mystery**

**(Book 2)**

**Bluestone Valley Publishing**

**Harrisonburg, Virginia**



**ISBN: 9781080992041**

## Acknowledgements

TO AKNOWLEDGE EVERYONE WHO MAKES IT POSSIBLE FOR ME TO WRITE A BOOK SUGGESTS THAT THE SIZE OF THIS DOCUMENT WOULD DOUBLE! I'VE OFTEN SAID IT TAKES A VILLAGE FOR ME TO GET ANYTHING DONE.

I WOULD ESPECIALLY LIKE TO THANK MARGARET DALY, PEGGY HYNDMAN AND SHERAN OBERHOLZER FOR ALL THE WORK YOU DO CLEANING UP MY GRAMMAR, MISTAKES AND CONTENT ERRORS. ALSO, I'D LIKE TO THANK MY BETA READERS FOR DOING THE SAME. I WOULD BE REMISS IF I DIDN'T ACKNOWLEDGE ERIC BLUMENSEN FOR HIS TIRELESS SUPPORT AND ENERGY HE PUTS IN TO HELP ME BECOME A BETTER WRITER.

I WOULD ALSO BE NEGLIGENT IF I DID NOT THANK ALL OF MY READERS FOR MAKING IT SO I CAN DO WHAT I LOVE TO DO! THANK YOU!

**Dedication**

THIS BOOK IS DEDICATED TO MY FRIEND AND ART BUDDY LAURALEA, A FANTASTIC ARTIST AND A TRULY GOOD FRIEND. YOU'LL SOON DETERMINE THAT IN THE ARTZY CHICKS MYSTERIES, LAURALEA PLAYS HERSELF AND I'M LILY LUCCI. OUR STORIES ARE OFTEN TRUE AND MUCH OF THE CONVERSATION IS WORD-FOR-WORD. WE HAVE ONE OF THOSE SPECIAL FRIENDSHIPS WHERE WE SPEND MUCH OF OUR TIME INSULTING AND BERATING EACH OTHER, WHILE IT'S TRUTH, A GREAT FRIENDSHIP EXISTS.

I HOPE YOU ENJOY THE MOST AWFULLEST CRIME OF THE YEAR!

# Contents

Acknowledgements........ 6
Dedication........ 7
Chapter 1........ 10
Chapter 2........ 26
Chapter 3........ 40
Chapter 4........ 47
Chapter 5........ 72
Chapter 6........ 78
Chapter 7........ 86
Chapter 8........ 97
Chapter 9........ 102
Chapter 10........ 115
Chapter 11........ 120
Chapter 12........ 128
Chapter 13........ 143
Chapter 14........ 155
Chapter 15........ 165
RECIPE........ 184
The Jewel Heist........ 188
Chapter 1........ 188
Chapter 2........ 201
Also by Judith Lucci........ 206

## Chapter 1

The July heat beat through the old hand-hewn logs at the 1700s log cabin that housed Artisan Galleries. It was hot and five of us sat around a crowded table as LauraLea, the gallery owner, wandered through her laundry list of announcements the artists needed to know. I generally don't think of LauraLea as someone who drones on and on, or purposefully tries to bore people, but today she was ready to pluck my last nerve. I was hot, thirsty and tired of sitting on my butt cramped in a corner by the fireplace. The window air conditioner grunted and hissed in its war against the outside heat. It was only 10:30 in the morning and the mercury had already blown past 90 degrees.

"Guys we've got to make a decision." LauraLea was getting provoked. Her green eyes flashed with impatience. "We've spent enough time on this. Let's vote." She glared at us over her stylish tortoise-shell reading glasses as she tapped her pencil incessantly on the table.

The lack of voices in the cabin said a lot. Only the hum, whirl, and groans of air conditioners and fans were audible. Five incredibly talented artists, better known as the Artzy Chicks, stared at each other without comment. And, if I must say so myself, this was most unusual. For all of us to stop talking at one time happens about as often as a snowstorm occurs during the Dog Days of Summer.  In other words, never.

I could tell that Diane, one of our older artists, main sales person and chief cook and candy maker, was about to blow. Diane likes to have everything perfect, even to the point where the pencils are lined up parallel to each other at each check-out area. She insists the shopping bags be stacked perpendicular for easy, quick plucking to bag art purchases. I'm not gonna tell you how she arranges the tissue paper we use to wrap the treasures the Artzy Chicks lovingly create. Diane likes everything ready at least thirty minutes before opening time. Diane is from New York State. She's a Yankee and she does everything in fast time. She's not used to the quiet, slow, genteel ways of the South, even though she's lived here for forty years. She's a retired elementary school teacher and trust me, she has no patience. She'll tell you in a New York minute that five-year-old kids used up her patience years ago.

I found the persistent tapping of LauraLea's pencil against her pad of paper a little unnerving. LauraLea, known to insiders as The Diva, is the owner of the Artisans Gallery Art and Gift shop located on Resort Drive at Massanutten, a five-star year-round glitzy vacation spot in the Virginia Mountains. She's an incredible artist and does the best wildlife drawings I've ever seen. She also uses pastels. We sell lots of her prints of bears, wolves, bison and most any other kind of wildlife or domestic animal.

The continued silence of my fellow artists irritated me, so I spoke up. I looked around at my good friends and fellow artists. I cleared my throat and stared at LauraLea.

"Here's the deal, LauraLea. No one wants to open earlier on Sunday. Even though we all work in the middle of Time Share Country, we'd like part of one weekend day off."

LauraLea glared at me. "Are you *sure*, Lily?"

"Yep. Positive." I could see the faint nods of the artists. "Right now," I said as I glanced out the window at the crowd gathering on the front porch waiting for us to open, and most likely, their first wine Slushee of the day, "I suggest we open the gallery."

Tammy Lynn, our country music queen and mixed-media artist shot me a grateful smile, rose from the table and moved into the wine tasting room where she opened six new bottles of wine for tasting. Everyone else scurried to their appointed places as well.

LauraLea shook her head. "I'm just gonna make the next major decision by myself and that will be to double art classes. How about that," she groused as she smirked at me. "It's hard to practice democratic principles when no one responds."

I watched as Vino, our gallery yellow lab rescue, moved from under the table where he'd been napping and walked slowly into the tasting room where he hoped a few drops of wine would fall his way. Vino was a drinking dog. He loved wine.

I nodded and took a seat behind the table where I was signing my books. "Good luck with that! I think you should do whatever you want to do, LauraLea. We all know you're going to anyway," I said with a smile and a short laugh, "so you may as well get on with it."

LauraLea grinned at me, "Aren't you glad we only have these meetings quarterly?"

"I'd rather you switch them to online annually," I grumbled. It was still before lunch time, so I tried to be politically correct. "I think quarterly is often enough. All of us would rather be creating art as opposed to being in a business meeting where you make all the decisions anyway."

LauraLea nodded and shot me a dirty look. "You wanna go to lunch? I'm hungry."

I checked my watch and shook my head. "Not now, LauraLea. Let me sell a few books first. You know I'm always good for lunch, just not right after I eat breakfast," I reminded her.

LauraLea shrugged her shoulders, stood and walked the short distance to the 'back room' where the Slushee machine, a 14-karat gold piece of molded plastic, churned wine, a sweet mixer and ice, and created what most people considered an amazing wine slushee for a mere price of six to ten dollars. The cost was sometimes by the size of the cup and at other times by whom was running the register.

I followed Laura and watched the machine turn over the ice and wine. It was a beautiful color. Since I'm a serious wine drinker, when I do drink, red and white wine slushees are hands down, not a choice for me. Yuk. But trust me, everybody else loves them, especially now during the dog days of summer. You wouldn't believe the number of people who visit us, browse the gallery and drink three or four wine Slushees as they sit on the porch and look at the mountains. Of course, that's perfect for us – especially if they buy books and art. After all, they're on vacation.

"Oh, you readers out there. It occurs to me that you don't know me. Let me introduce myself. My name is Lily Lucci. So far, you know I only like good wine... but there's more. I'm a child of the sixties, and a former business school graduate who turned into a nurse and a college professor. In the past few years, I've morphed into a medical thriller, crime, and more recently into a cozy mystery writer. I'm also an artist who spends lots of time painting and creating. To top it all off, I still see a few patients now and then and teach a class at my old University.

I live in the beautiful Shenandoah Valley of Virginia. Today, I'm with my friends at the Artisan Galleries located at Massanutten Resort, that is full-to-capacity. I sign books up at Massanutten Resort Conference Center on Monday afternoons, and down here at the Gallery on another day during the week.

LauraLea and I started the gallery as partners six years ago, but I left a few years ago when I retired from James Madison University. I'd decided I wanted to be a full-time writer. My duties here are limited which suits me fine. Since I frequently mess up the sales and inventory computer systems, I seldom have to cashier and I've messed up Diane's perfect pencil and paper system, so I'm not even wanted. I am rarely allowed behind the desk. My main job here is to smile and be nice. I also take care of the gallery critters, a drunken dog, a cat that scares snakes, and a possum with a sleep disorder. We have a few pet snakes once in a while, but I've put my foot down on that. Someone else can take the snakes to the vet. Every now and then the opossum, Gawd Almighty, will eat a snake which I think is just fine.

A screeching noise on the front porch startled me. I quickly ran to the door and looked out.

A middle-aged man and woman were almost to the top of the handicap ramp when the woman screamed and pointed, her voice shrill.

"Wilbur, what's that monster on the front porch? It looks like a prehistoric beast! It might attack us," she screeched, her voice loud and unpleasant enough to wake the entire mountain. Vino, who'd followed me to the door, turned around and ran into his hidey hole, under a table in the 'right room' as we call it. Vino often sleeps inside at night. He had it pretty good for an art gallery pet.

Wilbur, tall, with a bit of a paunch from living the good life, slowed his step, peered at the creature, took off his sunglasses and looked again. I opened the door, stood on the front porch and smiled.

"Good morning. I see you've noticed Gawd Almighty," I said pleasantly.

Wilbur spoke. "Why, why, that looks like – well, I hope it's a possum, an opossum," he said with a slight stutter. Possums sleep during the day, or, at least they're supposed to."

I nodded at Wilbur's surprised look. "You're absolutely correct. It’s a possum and, he's full-grown," I said proudly.

Wilbur's wife cowered back, "Is that beast going to attack us?" she asked, her voice loud and unkind to my ears.

I shook my head. "Nope, no way. He's as gentle as a lamb and much nicer than a Chihuahua I owned in my youth," I assured her.

The woman shot me a look of disbelief, so I walked over, sat in a rocking chair and called for Gawd Almighty, yes, that's our possum's name, Gawd Almighty, to come over and play. Immediately, as if on cue, Gawd Almighty, named by a man very much like Wilbur, left his corner space, came over and stood on his hindlegs, his paws resting on my knee.

Wilbur walked a little closer. "He's a big boy. Wow, he must weigh at least 25 pounds,” he said his voice loud.

I nodded and pushed back my short naturally highlighted frosted hair and said, "Gawd Almighty is almost 3 feet long and at his last vet visit, he weighed 27 pounds. So, yeah, he's big. He's a marsupial, the only one in North America."

Wilbur's wife looked at me like I was an alien.

"Marsupials carry their young internally as other mammals do, and then later in an external pouch called the marsupium, sort of like kangaroo do in Australia," I explained.

"Uh huh," she murmured as she gaped at Gawd.

"These creatures shared the earth with dinosaurs over 70 million years ago. While dinosaurs are extinct, opossums are still here, relatively unchanged. They must be doing something right, don't you agree?" I smiled.

The lady had totally missed my opossum 101 lecture.

“That... that thing goes to the vet? The woman had reached the second step of the gallery porch. She ogled me, still uncertain about approaching Gawd Almighty.

“Of course, he goes to the vet. All of our gallery animals go to the vet,” I replied crisply, as any good pet owner would.

"Will, will he bite me," she asked as she took a baby step forward.

I shook my head. "No, I promise, he won't. We have people that come here just to see Gawd Almighty every year. They even bring him food," I elaborated as I watched a beat up old green pickup truck pull into the gallery parking lot. I figured it was maintenance. I craned my neck to look at the bed of the truck. It looked like a bunch of cages.

"What does he eat?" Wilbur asked as he pulled out his iPhone to snap a picture.

"He likes a lot of stuff, but his favorites are snakes and fruit. At least that's what possums eat in the wild."

"Snakes, snakes, are there snakes around here," the woman said. "And he eats them?"

I nodded my head. This was my favorite part. I couldn't believe people came to vacation at Massanutten mountain, located in the middle of the George Washington Forest and didn't know we had snakes. I often wondered where they thought the snakes lived. "Yep he eats them every chance he gets. But he also likes oatmeal, cereal, birdseed and apple cores. Truthfully, he's not finicky," I announced.

Wilbur was about a foot from me by now and he was taking pictures of Gawd Almighty from every angle. "This is great, this is the coolest thing I've ever seen," he announced. "So far, this is the best part of my whole vacation," he said happily to the click sound of his iPhone.

I beamed at him. Gawd Almighty was cool but I was sure resort management would cringe at that statement. Most people loved the waterpark, the golf course, the ziplining, the pool, the classes… Anything but Gawd Almighty the resident possum that lived at Artisans Gallery.

I had noticed a second couple as they parked their car, their Cadillac SUV, and walked on the porch. The lady waved at me.

"Hello Ms. Lily. Wonderful to see you." She moved over and patted Gawd Almighty behind his ears. “Hi Gawd, you look great.”

"Hi Nina. I knew you were here this week. Great to see you, too." I watched Nina drop to her knees to be at eye level with Gawd. Out of the corner of my eye, I watched a man get out of the green pick up and head back towards the woods.

The first lady stared at Nina as if she were from outer space. "You'd better be careful. He might bite you," she said as her voice wavered.

Nina flashed her an irritated look and shook her head. "No, he won't. I've known him for years. He's gentle. And, he's special, wouldn't you agree?"

The lady shook her head. "I guess. But why?"

Nina's behavior betrayed her every thought and I'm sure she thought this lady was stupid. "I'm sure you know that possums sleep during the day. Gawd Almighty has a sleep disorder. He's one of the few possums around that are awake all day long," she said a happy light in her eyes. "He's famous in some circles." Nina continued to stroke Gawd Almighty as he waited for her to pull some snacks from her purse which she did."

"Well," I said. "Nina can tell you all anything else you need to know about Gawd Almighty. It's getting too hot out here for the likes of me so I'm gonna go in and hopefully sell some books."

Nina hollered at me and said, "Sign me three of the last one. I'm gonna give them as gifts."

I smiled. "I will, and I have a new one, too," I announced.

"Put it in my bag," Nina said as she continued to feed Gawd treats. I didn't know exactly what Nina did, but she worked in some capacity for the National Zoo in Washington, DC. I figured she knew a lot more about opossums than I did.

I heard barking before I reached the gallery door. Seconds later I saw Dr. Kenzie Zimbro's black lab Solomon, and our very own art gallery dog, Vino, run up the hill from the fishing pond. I knew they'd be wet and smelly. I was right. I chased them off the porch. It was too crowded with three adults, two dogs and Gawd. I knew Kenzie, our local medical examiner, would pull up in a couple of minutes. She always let her beloved dog, Solomon out a half a mile or so before the gallery where he met up with Vino.

## Chapter 2

Kenzie stood in the door of our tiny storage room which housed the refrigerator, a few shelves, the bathroom, a small table with several chairs. The sacred Slushee maker was there as well.

We loved Kenzie. In fact, we'd made her an honorary Artzy Chick. After all, she'd taken every class we'd ever taught at least twice. I knew when Kenzie was older and had more time, she'd completely develop the right side of her brain and become an outstanding painter. But for now, Kenzie had to entertain herself as medical examiner for Rockingham County and several other counties in the Shenandoah Valley. Kenzie was a phenomenal person and did great work. Her medical skills were the best, and we loved her dog, Solomon who seemed magical at heart. Most of us had a crush on Benson, her chief investigator. We all hoped Kenzie liked him too because it was crystal clear to the Artzy Chicks that he liked her.

"Who's dead?" LauraLea asked above the monotonous, humdrum of the Slushee machine. "Dead how?"

"LauraLea, honestly, how do you know someone is dead?" I ask impatiently. "Perhaps Kenzie just stopped by to visit."

LauraLea shook her head. "Nope, no way. I can tell by the way she moves. Her movements suggest she's in a hurry to get somewhere," Laura insisted.

Kenzie laughed. "LauraLea is right. I haven't visited the scene yet, but apparently, it's a guy, a Virginia Tech professor, a botanist. "

LauraLea shrugged her shoulders, a surprised look on her face. "Who'd murder a botanist? Don't they play around with leaves and stuff?" she asked as she poured a couple of bottles of wine in the groaning Slushee machine.

My eyes caught Kenzie's eyes and we both rolled them and gestured towards the slurping machine. In my mind and in Kenzie's, wine slushees were ludicrous and disgusting. In The Diva's eyes they were dollar signs.

"Oh, I don't know, but sometimes botanists do pretty cool stuff," Kenzie said as she rearranged her long dark hair in a scrunchie. The heat was stifling in the back room and the smell of wine almost overpowered me.

“Apparently, the botanist is pretty important. He rented the ginormous log structure at the tip-top of the mountain, The Mountaineer Conference Center, for a meeting."

"A conference? What kind of conference?" I asked as the drone of the Slushee machine began again.

"I don't know," Kenzie said. "But I can tell you, it's hotter than hades in here," she added, as she opened the freezer for moment and stuck her head in it. “Besides, the smell of wine is overwhelming!” she said with a smile.

"Want a Slushee for the road, Kenzie?” LauraLea teased. “It'll keep you cool on your way down the mountain," she snorted with laughter.

I could swear Kenzie got a shiver when she considered drinking a wine Slushee. I saw her wipe chill bumps from her forearms. “Nope,” she said with a grin. “I’ll stop at the 7/11 and get myself a grape Slurpee.  But I did stop by for a bottle of wine. Benson’s cooking Thai tonight. What do you suggest?”

LauraLea tossed her highlighted hair, pointed to me and said in her snotty voice, "Check with Dr. Lucci, the wine snob, Dr. Zimbro," she suggested with a smirk. "After all, she used to own a winery.”

I rolled my eyes again and motioned for Kenzie to follow me. "I’ve got just the thing. It'll be perfect with whatever Benson cooks," I promised.

Kenzie checked her watch. "Okay. Why don't you ladies come and join us for dinner," she invited. "I should be home by six."

I looked over at The Diva who nodded and said, "I don't know if I can stay for dinner, but I'm sure the two of us can come for drinks. How about that?" she replied as she winked at me, her green eyes flashing in anticipation.

"Works for me. Drinks only. That way I can get back to the 'Burg and let my dogs out before they flood my house," I nodded.

"Bring your own poison, Diva," Kenzie ordered. "I don't serve that sweet wine in my house," she reminded her.

LauraLea nodded. "I always bring my own. I don't like to share or run out of wine," she reminded us.

"We know," I said as I smiled at Kenzie.

Diane rang up Kenzie's wine but declined her invitation for drinks. I knew Diane's hip was bothering her. Otherwise, she'd never miss cocktails on Kenzie's deck."

I walked Kenzie to the door and watched her hustle Solomon, the love of her life, into her SUV. Kenzie never traveled anywhere without Solomon. Vino watched sadly as Solomon left. I looked over by the porch window to be sure Vino and Gawd Almighty had plenty of water. Vino looked up at me with a hang-dog look as Solomon breezed away in his mother's vehicle. I hoped Vino would cheer up soon. I reached down and rubbed his ears. I was sure there'd be a few other dogs down at the park for him to play with shortly.

I hoped no one gave him wine today. It was so hot it would affect him badly and besides, it wouldn't be good for his blood sugar. I shook my head. I wished Vino wasn't such a wino dog. It would keep my vet bills down and it was a tad embarrassing telling your world-famous veterinarian that your adopted dog, that didn't really live with you but rather at a local art gallery, had a drinking problem.

The vet had suggested some form of Antabuse, but it had never been tested on a canine group, so I politely declined. I'm not sure, to this very day, if he was kidding me or not. I returned to my book table, just in case anyone wanted an autographed copy of one my books. After all, I'd given up my 50% share of a gold mine Slushee machine to be a full-time writer. Most likely, before the day ended, LauraLea would make ten times more money on Slushees than I made in book sales.

"Lily, what are you doing?" I looked up and I saw the Diva standing over my author table. I had to hand it to the girl... or whatever she was. LauraLea looked great. The Diva was tall, amply proportioned lady with a set of teeth a spelunker would love. There was no question that her bright, white teeth could light the darkest cave on any mountain. In addition, she was a snappy dresser and almost everything she wore looked great on her unlike me who'd lost three inches in height in the last few years.

“I'm sitting here. Trying to sell books. What does it look like I'm doing?" I was grumpy most likely because I needed to eat.

"Good, let's go to lunch, Thunderbird or Ciros?" she asked. She named the two closest restaurants off the resort as she picked up my purse. I don't know what it was about LauraLea. She always had to pick up my purse and push me out the door. But she'd been doing it for years, so I guess it was her way. I also think it's her need for control and to push me around.

"Ciros," I chirped. "Might as well have the heaviest meal I can since we're stopping at Kenzie's for drinks."

LauraLea nodded as we fastened our seat belts. She quickly backed her new Lexus convertible out of the gallery parking lot. Clearly, wine slushees made her money. I certainly didn't have a Lexus. I was just a poor writer and retired college professor. I noticed the battered green pickup truck was still in the parking lot.

We quickly sped through the gate and LauraLea waved at several of the most incompetent police officers in the world. It irritated me that she stayed friends with the slugs on the Massanutten police force. Even though she despised them with a passion and they gave her tickets all the time, she managed to smile and flash her pearly whites several times each day. I simply ignored them. But, she had a business there and could need their help one day. Between you and me, she could catch a crook lots faster than they ever would. LauraLea packed heat and she was a great shot. She had a concealed weapons permit. I was a good shot, too but I didn't carry. I'd always been afraid I'd shoot myself in the foot. It just didn't seem right for me but I'm pretty cracker-jack on the range.

"Wow, look at all those police cars. I guess there's no police on the mountain," I said sarcastically as we passed the turn-off to the Mountaineer Conference Center. I noticed the bricked columns and metal gate of the estate sported yellow crime scene tape.

"The state police are there too," LauraLea noted. "This must be a pretty big crime," she ventured as she stared at the line of law enforcement vehicles parked single-file on the road leading to the top.

I shrugged my shoulders. "Either that, or the state police have figured out the Massanutten police don't know how to set up a crime scene yet."

LauraLea laughed. "Lily, you need to be a bit nicer to them and cut them a little slack."

"Me!" I said as I gave her a wide-eyed look. "I like them better than you do most of the time! Oh," I said as I counted the police vehicles. "I like them, I just don't think they know what they're doing. That's all," I said as I mumbled under my breath. "But, they're great at giving traffic tickets." I raised my eyebrow and looked at LauraLea who'd gotten her most recent ticket a few weeks ago.

She nodded as her face darkened in anger, "Yeah they are." Even glitzy, flirty Artzy Chick LauraLea hadn't been able to escape their speed demon traps. And, the last ticket she received had exponentially increased my knowledge of bad words.

We were in Elkton at Ciros Italian Eatery in no time. We walked in and the air conditioner blast in the face revived me. I was so hot I sneakily held up my arms to air out my pits. Then, out of the corner of my eye, I saw some hillbilly-looking dude over at the bar, complete with chains and tats, wave at LauraLea. *How in the world could she know him?* This guy looked like someone out of Deliverance.

The man scurried over, and I scurried off. He was fast for an old guy. His beard, that approached his belly-button, was stained with pizza sauce. Yeah. Pizza sauce. Not a pretty sight. I'd describe it as gross.

I about passed out when the man planted huge, wet, sloppy kisses on both sides of LauraLea's face. LauraLea smiled and backed up. I knew she wanted the floor to swallow her up. *Oooh. Gross.* They talked for a minute or so and then, well the guy enveloped her in a bear hug. I watched with dismay as the old guy pressed her flesh. LauraLea hated that kind of embrace. I knew she wanted to scratch his eyes out. I just hoped she didn't. I wanted to enjoy lunch without cops.

I turned away from the tawdry scene to sample a little wine they were serving with lunch. It was pretty good. Clean, clear and crisp, but I declined a glass although a quick look over my shoulder suggested that if the old dude didn't let go of LauraLea, I'd probably have to drink the bottle. The hostess wiggled her index finger at me and I fled to a booth.

LauraLea showed up a minute or so later, red faced, sultry and stewing with anger. I felt her fury surround me as her wrath heated up the air.

"Well, how was that and who was that? He obviously liked you," I snorted with laughter. "Obviously the old man thought you were his long, lost love or chick of the day," I giggled.

LauraLea shook her head and swallowed a few bad words. She shivered to try and shake the cootie's off her. "Oh, that's an old friend of my husband's father. He comes down the hill every once and a while for pizza. He lives in a holler somewhere on Lydia Mountain last I heard." she added, and she blew the man off. "His name is Ty and he's the Godfather and founder of the 'Hillbilly Mob' now better now as the Mountain Mafia."

I choked on my water. "Lovely," I replied sarcastically. The Mountain Mafia was the last thing I wanted to hear about at lunch. They'd been blamed for auto theft, home theft, convenience store robberies, a few murders and heaven knows what else. They weren't allowed on the mountain or anywhere near the resort because the management thought they'd rob the guests (which I agreed with). They also operated a lucrative chop shop that changes locations often. I shuddered as a mental image of the man's dirty beard jumped into my mind.

Lunch was good. We talked about art and planned an art exhibit. I ate a Philly steak and cheese and two of Lauralea's french fries. Yum. I even had them refill my drink cup and left with a go-cup of Diet Pepsi, my most favorite drink in the world. LauraLea consumed a mountain of a roast beef sandwich and all but two of her fries. We both left fat and happy.

## Chapter 3

"Where ya been, boy? I've been waiting for you all day," an angry voice spat at Peewee Flynn as the younger man got out of his pickup.

Peewee, who really wasn't short or small, shook his head. "I've been out looking for animals. Where you think I've been?" He eyed the old-timer and spat tobacco juice on the ground.

The old man looked less angry as he continued to whittle on a hunk of wood. "Okay, come on in here and show me what ya got. How many animals?"

"Get over here and look." Peewee unloaded the ten crates of animals he'd stalked and captured earlier in the day. He had a bunch of raccoons a huge jackrabbit, a couple of feral cats and some others.

"Wait a minute, old man," he said irritably, "let me unload these animals and get them out of the sun. Get over here and help me. It's too hot for them in this heat."

The old dude grudgingly stood up, came over and helped Peewee unload the cages into the shade of a cave that served as the headquarters for the Hillbilly Mob. Lots of bad business occurred in the cave and Peewee knew there were at least four or five skeletal remains in the back.

“What do ya care about the animals for,” the old man asked. “We ain’t gonna do nothing but kill em’ when it’s over.” The interior of the cave was chilly, and the twenty previously captured animals had settled into their skins.

*That ain’t happening.* Peewee checked out the animals. "You’re giving them water and food ain’t you? Last thing I need is someone down mountain tell me my animals look bad," he said through gritted teeth. Peewee didn’t much care for people, but he loved animals. He never hunted or trapped wild game. He planned to return each captured animal to the wild as soon as his hillbilly brothers were done with them. In the meantime, he wanted them fed and watered, especially in the heat.

Ty sat back down on his old metal lawn chair and picked up his knife. "They got enough, youngster. They'll be fine for the trip. We ain’t keeping them but another day." He picked up his knife and started to whittle at a piece of wood again. “What’d you care?”

Peewee nodded slowly. "I mean it, old man. Get up and help me. If I'm stopped for anything, and I do mean anything," he said as he got up close in the old man's face, "you’re gonna be dead in the water. Ya hear me?" Peewee's voice was rough. He was stressed as it was. It was hard enough for him to put the animals in the cave.

The old man glared at him. "Yeah, yeah, I hear you. I'll give them some more water in a little while," he said as he continued to scrape his knife against the wood. Ty’s voice was scratchy and hoarse from years of smoking and drinking moonshine. Peewee was pretty sure he’d burned through all the layers of skin in his food tube three or four times.

Peewee wasn't sure he believed him. "I got five gallons of water in my pickup. “Come on, man. Let's give it to ‘em now along with some corn so we can keep ‘em looking good for at least another 24 to 48 hours," he cajoled. Ty ignored him and continued to whittle his stick.

Peewee watched him for another minute, wiped the sweat off his high forehead with his hand, pushed his long hair back and walked towards the old man, and yanked the knife out of his hand. “I mean it. Get up, old man,” he snarled as he jerked the old man up from his chair.

Ty put down his wood, scratched his beard, fired off a few choice words and headed to the cave to help Peewee pour the water into thirty used plastic bowls. Ty was incensed as he watched Peewee pull on work gloves and place the bowls of water in the animal cages. The animals drank greedily as the two men chewed tobacco and watched.

Peewee gave the old man a furious glance, his lips pressed into a thin line. “You ain’t watered ‘em all day, have you?” Peewee cursed under his breath. “You’re a useless old man.” He glared at the old-timer.

Ty scowled at him. "What do you care? They’re watered now. Your happy the little animals have clean water," the old man snarled in a sarcastic voice. The older man glowered at him.

Peewee wanted to knock the guy into the hard earth. He looked at the old man’s nasty dirty hair and shirt. He nodded, "Yeah, I'm happy and you'll be happy when Hamn doesn’t shoot or beat us to death when he gets here. We got a lot of money resting on this job. Hamn’s gonna have everything we need today. Tonight we'll be messing with the animals and the cages again."

Ty shoved a wad of tobacco in his mouth. “What’s the plan for movin’ the critters out? Ya know? Man, it’s burning up out here,” he mentioned as he took out a large, dirty handkerchief and wiped his sweaty face.

Peewee shook his head. His long hair was plastered to his head from the heat. “Nah, not yet but if we go through the Massanutten police gate and they inspect the animals, they’ll confiscate them if any of ‘em look sick. Ya understand,” Peewee asked as he got into the old man’s face.

The old man grunted.

Peewee opened the igloo cooler and looked over at Ty. "Got any Mountain Dew?"

Ty shook his head. "Nah. You see a 7-Eleven around here, man?” he asked, a note of derision in his voice. “We're in the middle of nowhere. I got me some moonshine though if ya wanna snort or two,” he offered.

Peewee shook his head. “I need something to drink.”

“If you want to stay here and babysit the critters, I'll go get us a couple six packs, some ice and Doritos," he offered.

Peewee nodded and pointed with his finger. "Go. I'll stay here. I ain't got but a few more animals to pick up and we'll be okay," he said. Peewee sounded more confident than he felt. He'd decided that thirty animals were plenty but, just to be safe, he wanted to pick up at least 10 more. The Hillbilly Mob was known for their ability to be able to deliver anything to anyone at any time. And, they were all paid a ton of money for this skill set.

"How much is this job worth? What are we doing?" Ty asked as he raised himself up on his creaky old legs and stretched.

Peewee was surprised but shook his head. Ty had no idea what they were doing. Obviously, he was a nobody in the Hillbilly organization now. "I don't know for sure," he said as he stared at the ground. "But I heard it was a pretty penny. Probably more than we've made all year."

Ty nodded his head and shuffled to his pick-up. "I'm going out the back way, down the Western

Slope and head towards Harrisonburg. It'll take me longer, but I don't wanna go by the Massanutten police," he said.

"Good idea," Peewee agreed. "Them buggers always look at us like we're from another planet. Hurry back here with my drink, though. It's so hot out here I can hardly breathe." Peewee wiped his brow with a bandanna and headed towards the inside of the cave. At least it would be ground temperature in there. "Oh, stop by McDonalds and pick up a couple of Big Mac meals, would ya?"

"Yeah man, I hear you. It's boiling out here. Probably close to hundred. Can you imagine how hot it is down in the Valley?"

"Don't wanna," Peewee turned around and said. "It's the dog days of August."

## Chapter 4

I stood outside the gallery on the porch as LauraLea finished cutting off the sixty plus lamps that lit the gallery. Displaying art in a log cabin with only five tiny windows was a difficult task. A few years ago, we'd spent days and days searching out antique and unique lighting fixtures to illuminate our art. Still, it took about thirty minutes to cut the lights on and off every single day. Because, the cabin was old and historical, we weren't allowed to update anything. We struggled for five years to get hot water, so we knew there wasn't much hope of updating the electrical.

"I'm burning up. It's still hot out here," I hollered as I wiped my face with a wet paper towel. I'm sure I'd wiped off every speck of makeup I had on before 2 o'clock. It was so hot it was almost unbearable. It was the kind of sultry, August day when your clothes stick to you and you pray for the evening cool-off - only the cool-down never comes. For a few minutes, the thought of wine on Kenzie's deck wasn't so appealing. I longed for my covered deck at home next to my swimming pool. If I were going straight home, that's how I'd spend the evening.

"Yeah, it's still hot. I'm roasting," LauraLea said as she huffed and puffed out the gallery door. "Here, lock up for me, will you, Lily?"

I nodded. "I wonder where Gawd Almighty is? Vino's over here on the floor and Rembrandt's out back, but I don't see Gawd Almighty."

LauraLea glanced over to where Gawd normally slept. "Was he here when we got back from lunch? He's probably gone down to take a dip in one of the Springs. I've seen him swim in the Arboretum Springs before. I'm sure he's hot," she said as she wiped sweat from her forehead.

"You're probably right," I said. “I'd be in my pool if I was at home or sitting in my dark air-conditioned living room. Have you got your wine to take to Kenzie's?"

LauraLea nodded and flashed bottles of sweet red wine. "Yeah, I gotta couple of bottles. I'll be okay."

For the third time that day I got in LauraLea 's Lexus and we sped up the mountain towards Kenzie's house. Benson, her lead detective lived on the mountain too. We drove past his house, but his truck wasn't in the driveway.

"You think Kenzie and Benson are a couple yet?" LauraLea was a lot better at determining romance than I was.

LauraLea turned the air up on high and I savored the blast as it blew my naturally highlighted hair. "Boy, that feels good," I said. "Even the evergreen trees are beginning to look yellow," I observed.

LauraLea nodded. "Yeah, they are. I don't know about Benson and Kenzie being a couple. I hope so. I know he likes her, but I also know she's still grieving over her husband."

I nodded. "I know she is. She's such a smart girl. I hope somehow or sometime this turns into a romantic thing for them."

LauraLea nodded and she pulled in to Kenzie's driveway. Benson and Solomon met us at the car. "So, your cooking and you're on hostess duty too?" LauraLea laughed as she gave him a hug.

“Host duty,” Benson corrected as he hugged LauraLea back.

I leaned down to pat Solomon. He was an amazing dog. Benson gave me a kiss on the cheek.

"Kenzie was late getting home. She's in the shower. She was up there at the murder up at the Mountaineer Conference Center," Benson filled them in.

I nodded. "I can't wait to hear why someone murdered a botany professor." I could easily imagine someone murdering professors for their research but I'm sure teaching college had made me an incredibly boring person.

Benson grinned. He was so handsome with his white teeth, suntan and dark hair. I thought I was half in love with him myself. "Oh, Lily, you're gonna love this case. It's shaped up to be a pretty interesting case – full of surprises."

“Cool. I hate boring old murder. I love a case with a touch of the unusual.” I nodded as Benson picked up LauraLea's contribution of a couple of hunks of cheese and crackers she’d brought from the gallery. "I can't wait to hear."

The three of us walked into Kenzie's lovely home. Her house was simply but elegantly furnished in neutrals. She took advantage of all the natural light she received via skylights. The interior was dark and cool. We made our way to the kitchen where Benson poured us each a glass of wine and arranged the cheese on a platter.

Kenzie rushed to the kitchen and gave each of us a quick peck and greeting. "Hey guys." She turned to Benson and asked, "Is it too hot outside? Maybe we should stay inside here and wait until the sun sets," she suggested.

"I like that suggestion," I said eagerly. "I've been hot most of the day," I admitted.

"Okay that works for me," Kenzie said as she grabbed a glass of wine and the cheese platter. "Let's sit in the living room."

I took a quick look at Kenzie's photos on her mantle as I passed by. The picture of Kenzie, Solomon and Gabe, Kenzie’s deceased physician husband, broke my heart. I knew Kenzie still grieved for him.

LauraLea got to the point. "Well, tell us about the dead guy," she clamored as she tasted her wine.

Kenzie took a sip of wine and said, "It's turned out to be a potentially big case." Solomon came in the living room and lay on the ceramic tile in the foyer and eagerly watched the four of us.

"How so," I asked. "What exactly did this botany professor do?"

Kenzie pushed her damp hair off her face. I couldn't help but notice how in shape she was. I knew she worked out practically every day and that didn't count running the roads with Solomon. "He taught a couple of advanced botany classes at Virginia Tech, mainly plant science, but mostly he was a researcher. More of a research professor than a teaching professor. He was an expert in food science," she clarified.

LauraLea poured her second glass of wine and brushed her hair out of her face. "Okay, so what did he research?"

“He had a large government grant to study genetically modified foods. Specifically, corn. And, as it turns out, he's done the most advanced work in the United States and arguably in the world, on that subject."

"Corn, somebody gives you millions of dollars to study corn? That seems a bit excessive," LauraLea said.

"No, not really, not when you think about it, LauraLea," Kenzie said. "Think about it. We've been growing corn since the country was settled. Well, truthfully, I think the Indians taught us. Maize. The United States is also the biggest exporter of corn in the world. Think of what the perfect corn seed could do."

"Since it would be disease resistant, farmers wouldn't have to use any pesticides or fertilizers. Perhaps it could benefit farmers from having to rotate their crops, all kinds of stuff," I said as I reached for a piece of cheese.

LauraLea nodded. "Yeah. I suppose so. Maybe they could double or triple the size of their crops. Wouldn't that be great."

Benson came in from outside He was cooking something that smelled wonderful on the grill. He sat in the chair opposite me and asked, "What are you ladies talking about?

"Corn," Kenzie said. "I learned the botanist that was killed from Virginia Tech was a foremost expert in genetically modified corn."

Benson gave a low whistle. "That's a big deal," He was obviously impressed. "There's been a huge thrust towards the development of genetically-modified corn - for all kinds of good and bad reasons. I read somewhere they'd been developing an organic drought resistant and disease-free variety of corn. I remember reading that Agri-Tech, one of the biggest Agriculture corporations in the United States, had invested millions of dollars into corn research."

“Yep,” I said as I placed my hand over my stomach as it growled ferociously. “I remember Agri-Tech was one of the first companies to apply the biotechnology model to agriculture. They used the same techniques developed by biotech drug and pharmaceutical companies to develop genetically modified food.”

“Now, why would you know that, Lily?” LauraLea asked as she gave me a suspicious look.

“Because I used to teach a health safety course, I snapped at her. “Unfortunately, Agri-Tech didn't do well and became a corporate bad guy. A villain. The company was vilified all over the world, especially by the environmentalists and

Europeans," I added as my stomach growled again.

Kenzie grinned, "Lily, eat some cheese. Your stomach sounds like an eighteen-wheeler.

"Yeah. Do that, Lily, because you're grumpy," LauraLea accused.

I blushed with embarrassment. I felt my face turn red as I reached for another piece of cheese and a couple of crackers. "Okay," I agreed. "I'm pretty hungry. LauraLea never lets me stop and eat lunch. She's a slave-driver at the gallery." I grinned at LauraLea who gave me a dirty look.

LauraLea glared at me. "You ate like a hog today at lunch. We went to Ciros and you ate half of my French fries. Kenzie and Benson both know that eating is primary and foremost in our minds every day."

Kenzie and Benson laughed. "I'm sure you guys had lunch. I've hung out with the likes of you enough to know you never miss a meal."

LauraLea gave me a triumph look and I continued. "Anyway, I remember when Agri-Tech went from the future of American technology to being a joke on late-night TV. Who remembers the ‘frankenfood’ movement through Europe?”

LauraLea nodded. “Yeah. I remember that. It was vicious. It seemed to me that Agri-Tech was the only company that got blamed for making frankenfood although a bunch of other companies created it too.”

Kenzie nodded. “Yeah, that’s true. Frankenfood is simply genetically-modified food. But, honestly, Frankenfood was an albatross for popular fear and rage about everything,” she agreed.

I nodded. “It seems to me that food companies always have trouble and are a target for consumer rage. Remember the stuff with McDonalds with ‘Super-Size Me?” People get all worked up when they think their food could hurt them. Remember the stuff with Coke?”

“Yeah,” Benson observed. “Messing with someone’s food is different than having your car recalled or issues with General Motors. Food’s a personal thing,” he said with a smile.

“Yeah, it’s personal,” Kenzie agreed. “I love my food – my truck, I just want it to get me there… but then, I do like driving it,” she admitted.

"Well," LauraLea said. "The auto industry has been on the block a few times, too. Look at the issues Ford and General Motors have had in recent years with recalls."

I nodded. "That's true. But, I think the experience of eating is more personalized and the idea that someone has messed with your food, down to the very seed the farmer plants, angers people a lot more." I sat quietly and hoped my stomach wouldn't growl again.

"People just don't like to think that someone has adulterated, or mixed chemicals or messed with their food," Kenzie added.

"Well, yeah. It angers me," LauraLea admitted.

Kenzie nodded, "And the idea it could be toxic, well, that causes rage and works people into a frenzy." She paused for a minute to gather her thoughts and added, "However, I'm just as concerned about genetically modified organisms they feed animals and pets. They have done some atrocious stuff there," she said her face etched with anger. "It burns me up with some of the stuff they put in pet food," she glowered.

I was furious when I heard that. I'd played a huge part in the campaign against unsafe dog treats made in China. I shook my head angrily as I watched Kenzie's face flick rage.

"Oh my gosh, yes," LauraLea added. "If I hear anything like that again I'm gonna start a 'Mother's Against Bad Pet Food' which will make 'Mothers Against Drunk Drivers' look like a nice group of sorority girls." LauraLea's voice was bitter and her face red with fury. She'd lost a pet from substandard dog food and it'd take her ages to get over it. I reached over and touched her hand. I didn't want her to get too upset.

Benson changed the subject as he flipped through his phone. "It says here that in a recent poll in the *New York Times* that 25% of people surveyed believed GMO, or genetically modified foods are unsafe to eat to the point they're toxic. Of course, Agri-Tech suggests a lack of scientific evidence to prove this poll."

"What exactly is a genetically modified food?" LauraLea questioned. "Give me an example."

"Well, Benson said as he squinted his eyes and stared at his phone, "A *modified* organism is an organism whose genetic makeup has been changed in a laboratory using genetic engineering. Also, whatever they modify the food or plant with is not derived from biological organisms and not susceptible to genetic modification."

LauraLea nodded, "So, it's basically screwing with our food."

Kenzie nodded. "Yep, pretty much. That's it in a nutshell! They're basically modifying the food or plant with something that's not biological for a specific purpose," she added. "Perhaps they want a cheaper product or they better production, or, in the case of corn, a higher production."

My brain ticked away. "I think of it as tomatoes that never rot or get brown spots, or zucchini or yellow squash in the summertime. Lots of stuff we eat is modified. The US government doesn't require us to label genetically modified foods," I said. "I used to teach some of this content at the University in a health science class," I offered. "That's the only reason I know about it. Canada doesn't require labeling either but in Europe it's a different story. They mark food as genetically modified."

Benson nodded. "Yup, that's the truth. Regardless of all the flack and what people say and all the fuss, Agri-Tech has done incredible things for the world. They've created billions of dollars of food for the world with seeds genetically engineered to keep crops insect-free or make a crop immune to herbicides. Most farmers much prefer Agri-Tech seeds to competing products because they are easier and less costly to grow."

Kenzie was pensive. "Yeah, there's lots of good stuff about genetically-modified food. It wouldn't be America if we didn't meld science with foodstuffs. Agri-Tech, by marrying conventional breeding of seeds with genetic engineering has been able to produce more food for less money on the same amount of land." She paused and added, "It's hard to argue with that."

"I suppose," LauraLea said with uncertainty. "For me, if it ain't broke, don't fix it." Her face was stubborn.

Benson looked over his reading glasses at Kenzie. "The enemies of modified foods believe genetically-engineering crops has corrupted the earth. Some suggest genetic engineering has poisoned the earth."

"Yeah," I said. "They think genetically engineered seeds have blown all over the world and corrupted the earth with toxins, chemicals and pesticides." I hesitated, "Some folks, particularly the environmentalists, believe the seeds have blown all over the world and poisoned our land and water supplies."

We all knew Kenzie was a huge environmentalist, but she was also a scientist and she was pragmatic. I knew she was deep in thought.

"It seems to me the fact that this guy researched genetically modified corn must be considered as key in this case, especially with large amounts of money from Agri-Tech involved. Depending on his research, almost anyone would want his corn."

Benson nodded. "Yup, no question about that."

"I'll drive to Blacksburg tomorrow, to Virginia Tech and talk with his research assistants, colleagues and school administration," she said quietly.

The implications of this staggered me. It occurred to me that anyone in the world could want this corn... if it doubled or tripled the yield of corn. “This could be a very dangerous case, Kenzie. You need to be very careful,” I warned. “How much is the fifty pounds of stolen seed worth?”

Kenzie grinned. “I heard today that the seed alone is valued at over ten million. It’ll be much more than that once you add in the eight years of research.

Benson whistled and nodded. “That’s true, Lily. It could be a few half decent guys, or it could be the bad guys lined up for the secrets, patents and research.”

LauraLea frowned. “And fifty pounds of seed,” Laura reminded us. “How could anyone be good if they murdered someone? They’d have to be bad,” she insisted.

I nodded. "Stealing genetically modified plant material... and killing for it is pretty remarkable. Anything particularly interesting about how he was killed?"

Kenzie shot me a look. "Yeah. I’d say. He was shot in the back of the head. Execution style.

His death was short, quick and precise. Probably didn't take five minutes," she added as she looked at Benson.

"That it didn't," Benson agreed. "It was cold and brutal. A detached sort of crime. The man never had a chance to defend himself."

This information troubled me. "Was he alone? Was he up there on the top of that mountain by himself?" I asked. I'd been up The Mountaineer Conference Center several times. It was the most impressive log structure I've ever seen, complete with a bear trap on the front porch. It was massive. But, I was sure I never wanted to be up there alone. It was kind of lonely, spooky. When the wind whistled through the trees, I got chill-bumps. The structure, dark and imposing as it was, unnerved me. It was a bit eerie up there. Most people were afraid of the bear up there. I was more afraid of the Mountaineer Conference Center itself. The structure was in an open area and people could approach you from every direction. You'd never hear a thing because of the wind. It was just downright ghostly and unnerving.

"I wouldn't like to be alone up there," The Diva said. "It's pretty desolate and lonely. Who found him?"

"The hotel maids. It's likely he could've been up there for days if they hadn't come across him. He'd been dead since sometime last night," Kenzie reported. She stood to let Solomon outside. He'd come over and licked her fingers for attention. I couldn't help but admire his glossy, black coat. He was a great dog.

"So, what's he doing here at Massanutten? Why's he up at the Mountaineer Conference Center? What's his conference about?" I asked as the questions tumbled out. Something about this wasn't stacking up for my generally logical mind.

Kenzie nodded at Benson who responded. "Professor Rutledge planned to present his research findings to the executive board of the Agri-Tech Corporation and a few of their guests. The total number of people were not expected to top fifteen for the entire three-day meeting."

I nodded. "So, what's the motive for killing the good professor? Did they steal his slides or his notes?"

Kenzie shook her head. "Nope, they did not. That was the first thing we looked for. Professor Rutledge's computer was on the desk and appeared undisturbed. As a matter-of-fact, his computer was opened to his slide presentation. Everything seemed to be in order," Kenzie added as she handed her glass to Benson and he refilled it from the chilled carafe on the coffee table. “The FBI confiscated his computer.”

LauraLea looked as confused as I felt. "Couldn’t they have copied his files on an USB drive? So, what's the deal? Do we have any idea who killed him?”

Kenzie shook her head. “I don’t, at least not yet. Do you guys, Benson?”

“Not really,” he said. “We have a couple of leads. We’re working with the state police and the FBI. We should have more tomorrow.”

LauraLea frowned. “It seems to me he had something someone really wanted. It certainly wasn't a random murder, not up there in the middle of nowhere," she said as she examined her perfectly polished nails. “I just don’t get it.”

"That's true – certainly not random and we wondered the same thing. We looked around and couldn't find any motive for murder, at least not initially," Kenzie said.

"Did you check his hotel room, in his luggage? Was there anything there that gave you an idea?" I asked.

Benson nodded. "Yeah, there's several things actually. It was clear to me that the murderer went to his room before he approached the professor in the conference center. The murderer left us a nice trail of muddy boot prints that extended from Professor Rutledge's room almost to his body."

"Mud? It's so dry here. We haven't had any rain for days. Where'd this person bring the mud from?" I wondered aloud.

Kenzie grunted. "Now, that's a very good question. There were no tire tracks we could see so we figured he probably walked up there from somewhere."

LauraLea scowled. "But that place is in the middle of nowhere. It's at the tip top of a mountain. Where would the perps come from?"

Benson laughed. "We don't know that yet, LauraLea. However, I think there was one murderer, but I suspect he found a road almost to the top. Perhaps he jumped out of the vehicle and walked the last mile, so he could catch the professor alone."

LauraLea nodded. "Yeah. Maybe. But I still don't understand the big deal about genetically modified corn. Why would someone murder someone else over corn secrets or a corn formula?"

Benson stood. "Now, LauraLea. There are a lot of reasons for that. Let me open another bottle of wine and I'll tell you my theories when I return.

LauraLea nodded "Sounds like a plan to me."

I looked at Benson as he looked down at LauraLea. I couldn't help but notice how handsome he was. His dark hair was perfectly cut, and his muscles bulged under his white knit shirt. There was nothing shabby about him. If I were a lot younger, I'd chase the good-looking, North Carolina law enforcement myself.

Benson returned with a new bottle of wine. He filled my glass and Kenzie's glass. LauraLea was still drinking her sweet red wine! Yuk. "Thanks, Benson. This wine is every bit as good as I remembered," I said as I took a sip and nabbed a couple more pieces of cheese.

"I agree," Kenzie said with a grin. She looked over at Benson. "We should keep this one on hand... as an everyday wine," she winked.

"I will," Benson promised as he turned towards LauraLea. "Consider the perfect corn crop. Corn that would grow under any conditions, too much rain, a late spring hard freeze or drought. Corn that would grow without pesticides and fertilizers and chemicals. This corn could maybe yield twice as much per acre. What a dream that would be for farmers."

LauraLea nodded. "Yeah, I get that."

Benson nodded. "Plus, you gotta remember that corn is the biggest crop we produce in the United States. We ship it all over the world. So, you can only imagine the benefits of the perfect corn seed with high yields, right?"

"Sure," she said as she filled her glass.

"Plus, isn't it true that farmers can't keep their corn from year to year like they used to a long time ago? Corn seed must be purchased every year now," I said. "That's an added expense to them."

"Yeah, it is. A huge expense," Kenzie agreed. "That's why they need a good yield simply to cover expenses."

"Anyone could want that corn. Another US corporation that's a competitor with Agri-Tech or foreign corporation... even terrorists," Laura considered. "Russians could get their hands on all the research secrets of genetically modified corn, think about the impact that could have economically and globally."

Benson played with his wine glass and balanced it on the coffee table. "We're pretty sure Professor Rutledge wasn't killed for his slides or his research notes."

"So... Why did they kill him? Why did they execute him, so to speak?" LauraLea questioned, her voice unsure.

Kenzie smiled and said, "For his corn. He was executed so the perp or perps could steal the fifty pounds of genetically modified corn he brought with him." Solomon gave a short bark outside and she opened the door and let him in.

I shook my head as my mind swirled with the possibilities of a perp with fifty pounds of corn. "That's pathetic. They murdered him for fifty pounds of corn. Is that what you're saying?" I asked.

Kenzie nodded. "Yep, Fifty pounds of corn. We found the two burlap bags he carried it in from Virginia Tech outside the Lodge, on the deck."

LauraLea’s green eyes were wide open. "That's pretty unbelievable. I'd never think fifty pounds of corn would be a motive for murder."

“Not just a murder, an execution,” I reminded her.

"Well, it is in this case," Kenzie said. "But to solve the crime, we’ve got to figure out what's so special about this corn. Why was it worth killing Professor Rutledge."

Solomon barked sharply and ran to the window.

"Oh, it must be Angie and Fred. They’re stopping over for wine and dinner,” Kenzie said with a smile as she rose and went to the door.

LauraLea grinned. "I haven't seen Angie for a month or so, not since the Fourth of July. I'm sure she'll update us on what's going on up at the conference center on this side of Massanutten," she said as she nodded towards the ski slopes hotels and convention centers that comprised a large part of the resort.

"No question, Angie knows when a fly lands around this place. Let's have one more glass of wine and let her bring us up to date," Kenzie suggested as she opened the doors to Angie's squeals and Fred's low voice.

Fred was Kenzie's assistant and morgue technician. He had one of the best personalities I'd ever been around. And, Angie was one of the best gals around. I looked at LauraLea and signed I'd like to stay.

## Chapter 5

I hugged everybody goodbye as LauraLea switched on her car lights. One thing about Massanutten Mountain is that it's dark as pitch once the sun goes down. Kenzie promised to stop by the gallery in a day or so and update us on the 'Corn Murder' as we had named the case surrounding the death of Dr. Rutledge. Benson and Solomon walked me to the car. I reached down and gave Solomon a hug and kiss on the top of his head.

LauraLea was quiet as she drove down the mountain. I was glad. Even though we both knew Massanutten mountain like the back of our hand, we were never sure if the timeshare people and hotel guests knew how to navigate the twisting curves and hairpin turns on the mountain. It wasn't unusual for someone to slam on their brakes and a five-car pile-up would be the result. Plus, you never knew how quickly someone would pull out in front of you. Regardless of what anyone said, driving in the mountains was an acquired skill. It wasn't something you drove up from the flatlands and did well without exercising a little caution.

LauraLea interrupted my thoughts. "I'm gonna stop at the gallery and pick up my painting bag. I think I'll stay home tomorrow and do a couple of drawings. I don't want to sweat up there five days in a row," she said. LauraLea said this all the time and always showed up the next day.

"Good idea," I agreed. "I want to see if Gawd Almighty came back and got in his cage under the front stoop." It was interesting – and kind of cool, that Gawd Almighty, our possum with a sleep disorder, preferred to sleep in a cage at night when the rest of his ilk were out wandering. We'd gotten him a large dog kennel a few years ago. Of course, the door wasn't latched, but for some reason it gave Gawd a sense of safety and protection. And who was I to question an opossum with a sleep disorder?

LauraLea nodded. "Yeah, good idea. He wasn't on the porch when we left. Chances are he's gone to bed in his crate," she said. She shook her head, "I still can't believe we have a possum that lives on our front porch that has a sleep disorder." She giggled.

I laughed too, even though Gawd Almighty had been around for years, it was only in the past four years or, so he'd let us get close and touch him. Gawd was insightful, cautious, and wary, like most opossums, a fact that probably enabled the species to survive since the dinosaur age. Certainly, lots of other animals had died off or their species were extinct. Opossums are just plain smart and that's that.

"We should check Vino's water, too. I have no idea how much wine he drank today so he could be dehydrated from that. Plus, it's so hot!" I said. "I wish people would stop giving him wine," I protested. "It's so hot out here Gawd, Vino, and Rembrandt drink water like it's going out of style," I observed.

LauraLea nodded, "Yeah, I asked two people today not to give him wine. They think it's funny but it's dangerous. I left the spigot running at a trickle on the left side of the cabin." I'm like you, it's so hot I don't want them to dehydrate," she said as she turned into the driveway of the gallery. Her headlights illuminated the front of the cabin, I could easily see that Gawd Almighty wasn't in his cage. A pang of fear shot through my belly. Gawd Almighty was a creature of habit and he generally returned to the deck where he stayed until it turned dark and he went in his crate to sleep. "He's not there," I said to LauraLea. I hope my voice wasn't too anxious.

"I've got my flashlight. I'll look out back for him after I get my easel and my art supplies," she promised me.

I nodded and switched the Sirius radio station. I loved Bruce Springsteen just like anyone else, but I turned the dial to light classical. Besides, I wanted to think about Professor Rutledge and the genetically modified corn that had probably cost him his life. Plus, I was a little worried about Gawd Almighty although, for all I knew, there were plenty of nights he didn't sleep in his crate. After all, I wasn't at the gallery every night to check out his sleep preferences. The thought that he could have a girlfriend crossed my mine and I smiled to myself.

I saw a light in the woods behind the cabin. I figured it was LauraLea, so I closed my eyes and listened to the quiet calm of outdoor insects and the Echo Symphony. LauraLea had the air conditioning on, but it was still warm in the car. I continued, with my eyes closed, to listen to the symphony and wished for hope and world peace, and a cold front. It had become uncomfortably warm in the car when I heard the trunk open and felt LauraLea drop her art bag in. That bag was loaded with so much paint, paper, brushes and painting mediums it probably weighed over thirty pounds. The car groaned when she dropped it in.

I looked up at her when she opened the door. She shook her head. "I didn't see Gawd Almighty outside. I looked all around back and side of the cabin."

I nodded but remained silent. I was bummed.

LauraLea reached over and patted my arm. "I'm sure he's okay, Lily. After all, he is a wild animal that's survived since prehistoric times. There's every chance he's down by the pond. It's still pretty steamy out here for nine a clock."

"Yeah, it's still really hot. I sorta hope he has a girlfriend," I said with a smile. "When's that cold front coming through. This heat is oppressing," But what really bothered me was the missing opossum.

LauraLea backed out of the parking lot and said, "Look, do you see that light in the woods? The light behind the cabin? I noticed that when I was out back."

I strained my neck and looked back. "Yeah. I saw it when you were in the gallery. I thought it was you. Maybe we should stop on the way out and tell Massanutten's finest," I suggested. I noticed the pickup truck in the parking lot.

LauraLea gave me one of her 'What planet did you come from' looks. "There's no way I'm stopping at the police station. They'll tie us up forever and do nothing."

I nodded. She was probably right.

It was a crackpot idea.

## Chapter 6

It was morning. I'd had a restless night. I couldn't sleep and woke up several times as my mind jumped to Gawd Almighty and where he was. I'd hoped he was back home entertaining the resort guests on the front porch, but I knew in my heart of hearts he wasn't. It was shortly before noon when I got my first phone call from LauraLea telling me that Gawd Almighty still hadn't shown up.

"Well," I said. "I've written my first 3000 words today, so I think I'll come over there and look around for him a little bit. Aren't you busy? I thought you were 'doing art' this morning."

I could hear LauraLea multi-tasking and I knew I had about one-eighth of her attention. Of course, we were never busy enough for LauraLea – even if we'd filled the Slushee machine four times in a day and sold five hundred dollars of the sickening sweet wine drinks.

"Yeah. No art for me today. We're busy, but Diane and Tammy Sue are here. Come on and we'll look for Gawd and then maybe have some lunch up on the mountain," she invited just before she dropped her cell phone and crashed my eardrums.

Patient person I am, I hung up the phone and waited for her to call me back. It took about five minutes. “Yes. Are you back?” I asked in my smiley, happy, ever patient voice.

“Sorry ‘bout that. I dropped the phone. Come on in. We’ll look for Gawd,” she said breathlessly. I figured she was on a ladder. She was always breathless when she was on a ladder hanging art, but she always denied it. I personally think she’s scared of heights.

“Get off the ladder. I’ll be there in a bit and I’ll hang the pictures,” I promised as I hung up the phone and turned to look at my own five dogs who lay on the floor. Each of them had their eyes trained on me. They knew something was up.

I stood and stretched, and my five dogs stood and stretched. I am the proud owner of the Ling Ming family, a collection of Shih Tzu’s who love me without prejudice or reservation and I love them back. Sam, Sue, Sheera, Sophie, and Lotts are my furry non-judgmental family members. They don’t need prom gowns, fancy hair-dos, giant legos or college funds. They just want me... and Canine Carry-out treats. They followed me into the kitchen and waited patiently as we paused at the treat bag. I took out five pieces of duck jerky and they followed me outside where they had their treats while I hosed down the flowers and the potted plants. It was hot and I knew my blooms wouldn't make it through the day without a couple of trips from the water hose.

I sat in the shade and watched my dogs stare at me like I was an idiot for sitting outside. One thing about Shih Tzu's, my breed of dogs, is they hate hot weather, so they take care of things quickly outside, so they can beat feet back into the cool air-conditioned house.

Thirty minutes later, I hit Massanutten Mountain and started the climb. I noticed there were still several police cars at the bottom of the road that went to the top to the Mountaineer Conference Center. I wondered if Kenzie was up there. Maybe, after LauraLea and I searched for Gawd Almighty, we'd see if she wanted to grab a burger somewhere. Kenzie often worked out of her home although her real office and her morgue were in Roanoke Virginia. Unless she was doing an autopsy or attending meetings, Kenzie was generally on the mountain. But, of course, she had driven to Virginia Polytechnic Institute in Blacksburg, you know, The Hokie Nation, where the late Professor Rutledge had taught.

Vino met me at my car. His muzzle was wet, so he'd been drinking water. He licked my hand in greeting. He was panting heavily so I decided to let him in the gallery to cool off. That'd probably limit his wine intake as well. I noticed LauraLea had plastered another sign on the door that clearly read, **Do NOT Give the Dog WINE! PLEASE.** I shook my head. I hope it worked.

The gallery parking lot was full. A reader stopped me on my way in and asked me to sign a couple of my books. I never tire of signing books for people that are kind enough to purchase and read them. They give me the energy to continue.

“Hey Tammy," I smiled as I greeted her. Tammy was in the tasting room drying wine glasses. She was absolutely the most put together person I knew. Her dark hair was always in place, she never looked hot or sweaty like I always did. Her clothes were perfect, and she had more statement necklaces than eBay! She always looked fantastic, kind of like she jumped out of a fashion magazine. The best part of

Denease though, was the fact that she was one of the nicest people I've ever met."

She shook her head and rolled her eyes. "I've poured and sold so much wine I can't believe it. Look out there," she said as she pointed out the window. There were a half-dozen people drinking glasses of wine, and a dozen or so folks slurping down ghastly wine slushies under the tree. Of course, it's only fair that I say that everyone in the world, except you and me, love the wine Slushees." Denease smiled her lovely smile and winked at me.

I shook my head. "Well, that's LauraLea's million-dollar Slushee machine at work," I said with a smile. "It's good. If people drink Slushees, you'll have a job. Plus, LauraLea won't have to worry about paying the rent, and I'll be able to sign a book now and then."

Denease nodded as her big brown eyes studied me. "I suppose you're right," but rolled her huge brown eyes again. "How do these people drink wine in the ninety-degree heat? If I had more than one glass, I'd pass out!"

I nodded and shook my head. "Beats me. Where's LauraLea? We're supposed to go look for Gawd Almighty."

Tammy's eyes softened. "Poor Gawd. I'm so sorry he's missing. I have no idea where that dear thing is," she said sadly. "He'll turn up. Sometimes he runs off, but he always comes back." Her voice was hopeful as she smiled at me and touched my hand. Her voice was gentle and hot tears filled my eyes.

"I'm gonna stick Vino inside so he can have a nap in the air conditioning. I'm afraid all of those people will give him wine Slushees and make him sick," I said as I turned my back to leave.

"Lily," Tammy Sue said softly, "Gawd will come back, I'm sure he will. Probably soon," she added in her kind voice.

I nodded slowly. "I suppose. I'd just like to see him," I said stubbornly. I felt my eyes burn with unshed tears, but I held them back. "Where's The Diva?"

Tammy flashed her long eyelashes toward the front room. "LauraLea's in the right room hanging paintings."

I nodded and smiled. "Thanks, Tammy. Do me a favor," I asked. "Keep your eyes on Vino once he goes back out. Also, could you remind the guests not to give him wine? He is, after all, a dog," I said indignantly. "They may think a drunk lab is funny, but it's not when it makes him sick and dehydrated!"

Tammy touched my hand again. "I promise, Lily. I'll watch out for him," she assured me as she turned to greet a customer.

I forced my way through the crowd waiting to pay for their Slushees in the pay line. Diane was ringing up sales. One thing about Slushees, you didn't have to wrap them, so Diane's pencils and tissue paper were in perfect order. She waved at me as I walked by on my way to the right room.

LauraLea was on a ladder. "Are you sure you have time to search for Gawd?" I asked. "It's pretty busy in here."

"Are you serious?" She glanced at Diane and Tammy. "Yeah, they're okay. I gotta get outta here. This place is driving me nuts. Besides, the morning rush will slow down in a little while and everybody will head for the pool. We'll be busy again about 3:30 just like it always is during the summer."

I grinned. "Just like it is every summer. That's for sure." I changed the subject. "I called the police last night about the light we saw. I don't know if they investigated it or not," I said. "Nevertheless, I want to go back there first."

"Sounds good to me," LauraLea said. "We'll search on foot behind the gallery first. Twenty minutes later LauraLea and I were out searching for Gawd Almighty and it was hotter than Hades.

## Chapter 7

LauraLea and I spent over an hour in the wooded area behind the gallery. Bugs feasted on us and sweat bees were everywhere. But, there was no sign of Gawd Almighty. One thing we did find were some interesting indentations and flattened areas in the grass on the forest floor.

"Whew, it's getting hotter out here," LauraLea said as she pulled her long shirt away from her body and pushed her highlighted red hair out of her face. I nodded and wished I had a spray bottle of water. She didn't have to convince me. I was cooking. It wasn't unusual to have people walk back behind the cabin since it was the Rockingham Springs Arboretum, but it was too hot now. We'd had a lovely spring border for a while and then a few summer wildflowers. We also had a nice flat walking path where almost anyone could walk quietly and peacefully in the evening. The path led down to the Rockingham Springs, an underground spring. People used to come and bathe in the waters from Richmond, Washington and the northern states to ease their aches and pains. There used to be a posh hotel there until the 1940s where the rich would come and 'escape' the dirty air of the big cities to gain some fresh mountain air. The hotel was long gone now.

Laura and I continued to go deeper and deeper into the forest and the path wasn’t flat or kind. It was downright dangerous and rocky. I almost went down on all fours when I tripped over a fallen tree.
Laura screeched at me to be careful.

"Lily, look over here at all of these areas in the tall grass where it’s been pushed down flat,” LauraLea pointed in the distance. “It looks like somebody set something up here," she observed as she noted a puzzled look on my face.

I bobbed my head up and down. "Yeah, I've noticed those ever since we left the wood line. It looks like something was arranged, but I don't know what it could be. Did we get any notifications from the police about anything going on back here? Maybe a celebration or something?"

LauraLea shook her head. "Nope. I can't imagine what the resort would be doing this deep in the woods. It doesn't seem likely they would've planned an activity this time a year – not as hot and buggy as it's been."

I nodded. I personally couldn't imagine a kid today walking in the woods when it was 95° but then, I could be wrong. I spent every waking moment of my summer outside when I was a kid. I shrugged my shoulders. "Perhaps the Mountain Adventure Club, the ones that set up the nature walks, set up some sort of a nature obstacle course for kids, like a nature trail or something? Maybe they were looking for rocks and fauna and flora. Heck I don't know." I said impatiently. It was getting hot and a fly buzzed in my ear.

“Maybe,” LauraLea agreed “but I seriously doubt it. Too many snakes and stuff down here for a nature camp.”

“I thought that was what a nature camp was,” I said indignantly. “That’s what I did at nature camp. I even pinned the bugs I caught to cardboard with straight pins,” I said as I smiled at the memory although I’d thought it was pretty gross at the time.

LauraLea smirked at me “You were such a cruel little kid. I can see you now sticking bugs in alcohol and formaldehyde and stuff. Probably studying them like some little Einstein in glasses,” she teased. “I saw those pics of you when you were little.”

I laughed. "That's exactly what I did. I confess those scientific crimes. I loved it. There was something therapeutic about sticking bugs with straight pins.  I don't guess kids do that anymore. They probably look at them on the internet and print out a picture," I commented as I shook my head. "They miss so much being plugged into those video games, DSs, and phones."

LauraLea scowled at me. "You're disgusting, but it probably turned you into a crime writer. "But," she said as she looked around the clearing, "I don't think it was a kid's camp. Besides, if we'd had a kid's camp behind us, we'd have seen them in the gallery. Plus, Diane would have a heebie-jeebies fit with all those kids coming in the gallery with dirty hands. Plus, they'd want to use the bathroom and you know they'd clog up the toilet. Diane would've gone nuts."

"Yeah, she would," I agreed. "Diane isn't much on kids in the gallery, is she?"

LauraLea laughed. "Let's just say Diane is big on order. Everything in its place, stuff like that. You know how totally obsessive she is about stacking the wrapping tissue and bags."

I laughed. "And lining up the pens and paper. She's totally obsessive about that... which is good because we aren't."

LauraLea nodded. "Yeah, our brains tend to stray to the right. We're not that good with order. Diane sure doesn't have a lot of patience for a retired kindergarten teacher," she admitted.

I snorted. "That's exactly where her patience went. If I'd taught five-year-old kids, I wouldn't have lived to be this old," I declared honestly. "I'd have died in jail. I love kids, just not every day."

LauraLea's beautiful green eyes glistened in the sunshine. "Yeah, I remember that summer you and I planned a season of kid's craft classes. We had planned classes the entire summer. We were so excited..." she squealed with laughter. "How long did we last?" she prodded, a devilish look in her eyes.

I smiled. "I think our first and last class was on Mother's Day. We just couldn't handle those nine kids painting those flower pots with Tempera paint and then filling them with dirt and a half-dead flower," she laughed at the memory. “I hope those Mother’s treasure those pots for years to come because it took at least five years off my life!” I giggled. “I guess that wasn’t much of a summer for kid’s art, was it?” I said with a sheepish grin.

I shook my head. “Do you remember when two of them broke the blooms off their flower. I thought you were gonna lose it,” I laughed so hard tears ran down my face.

Laura laughed. “Yeah. I remember. We didn’t even make it to summer.” She stopped and looked at the ground. “Look, Lily, it looks like someone has been moving stuff here.” She pointed to the ground. “It looks like something has been pulled or pushed up the hill,” she said as she bent down and looked at the dry, rutted tracks in the earth.

I nodded “Yeah. It looks like they pulled something up the hill.” I stared at the area. The grass on the forest floor was matted down and I could see where something heavy had pressed into soil. I didn’t know what it was or could have been. I looked at LauraLea. “What do you think it was?”

LauraLea shrugged her shoulders and wiped the sweat off her face with the back of her hand.

" No clue, but this is getting old. Let's head back, get back in the Explorer and we'll go look around the ponds. Maybe he's around there," she suggested. "For all we know, he's swimming with some beavers somewhere," she said as she tried to cheer me up.

I nodded but I wasn't hopeful. Somehow, I knew that if Gawd Almighty was close to home he'd have been there. I realize he's only a possum, but he's got a lot of good sense. I watched him through the years and he seemed to know who to trust and who not to trust. I watched him as he looked at people when they walk up on the porch and gawk at him. He'd take off like a lightning bolt if he decided he didn't like someone. He'd run for cover and reappear later. I looked up at LauraLea.

"Sounds like a plan. At least we'll be in the air conditioning," I said as I fanned myself with my hand. "It's pretty miserable out here and I've gotten fly bites already." I was full of complaints and my whining hurt my own ears.

LauraLea grunted. "I have a trillion bites."

The two of us emerged at the edge of the woods about fifteen minutes later. Both of us were ringing wet with perspiration. I turned to

LauraLea and said, "I don't know about you, but I'm fried – both body and brain."

LauraLea nodded and pushed her normally elegantly styled, now sweaty hair back from her face, "I won't argue with that. Get in the car," she ordered.

"Get that air conditioning on," I whined as I slipped in the passenger's seat and faced all the vents on me. I'm oldest, so I should need the air the most," I reminded her. LauraLea was one of those people who always wanted control over as much as she could control, so she always drove. I always complained about it but truthfully it didn't bother me a bit. I rather liked it. Her chauffeuring me around, that is.

LauraLea jumped in the car and immediately turned the air-conditioning vents back toward her. I gritted my teeth and claimed the ones on my side and turned them on me. We creeped along the side of the pond near the picnic area. We went so slow I expected the Massanutten police officer, Dick Derek, who I'd seen working the desk, to come over and investigate us. But, I knew Dick would never come out of his airconditioned cubbyhole on such a hot day. If he had ventured out, I'm positive he'd give us a ticket for driving too slowly.

"You see anything?"

I shook my hand. "Nah. Not a thing. Why don't we drive down to Woodstone Recreation Area and talk to the people down there? I'm sure a couple of them know Gawd Almighty by sight. They would've noticed him if he'd been down on that side the mountain."

LauraLea nodded. "Good idea. The thing about Gawd Almighty is people would notice him. You never see "possum" out during the day. I would've thought someone would've called us if they'd seen him."

I nodded. "Let's stop by and asked the police. I think that if people didn't recognize him as a possum, they'd call the police."

LauraLea shook her head. "Who knows, I have no idea."

"I... I just hope no one hurt him!" My heart cringed. *There. I'd said it.* Perhaps it would come true now that I'd said it. *Was that flawed thinking or what*? I often reverted to my foolish childhood games in times like this.

LauraLea shot me a look, "I hope no one hurts him either, although he's a pretty smart possum and is intuitive too. Chances are he's okay," she added in her reassuring voice.

I turned my head the other way when LauraLea pulled up to the police department window. I didn't recognize the guy on duty. He must be a new hire. Dick Derek was probably on break. We seem to see a lot of new hires at Massanutten in the police department. Problem is, the good policemen leave, and the crap ones stay around forever.

I watched LauraLea ask the guard about Gawd and scribble down her phone number and give it to him. Both of our phone numbers were plastered all over police headquarters. LauraLea's number is there because she owns the gallery. My number's there because I used to own the gallery and they couldn't get it through their thick police heads that I no longer did. I still got Laura's emergency phone calls. All the time. She's always out having fun and I'm home working.

LauraLea scooted through the police gates onto the mountain road where she immediately picked up speed. The air conditioning felt great on my hot, sticky, dried up face.

“Well, that’s done,” LauraLea grinned. “See how easy that was?”

“Yeah, but only because he kept trying to look down your blouse,” I said sullenly.

LauraLea looked down. “No, he didn’t either,” she argued as her green eyes flickered angrily at me.

I ignored her. “I’m pretty tired of summer. I'm ready for the fall, cool weather, mums and pumpkins” I said wearily.

LauraLea nodded. “Yeah, I know. I’m right behind you there, sistah.”

## Chapter 8

Hamn Slot, the boss of the Hillbilly Mob, pulled up as near the cave opening as his massive black truck would allow. Peewee peered at him from the darkness of the cave. Hands down, Hamn's truck was the hottest thing Peewee had ever seen. The truck was an old, jacked-up Dodge Ram with dually wheels and a Cummins diesel. It had two big stacks behind the driver's cab that Hamn filled with some illegal additive. The truck blew thick black smoke all over the roadways and enraged the environmentalists around. His favorite pastime, when he wasn't planning muggings, mayhem and robberies, was to ride through the University districts and piss-off the faculty. Hamn hated environmentalists. In fact, Hamn hated most everyone – especially if they were going to try and tell him what to do. The truck also sported the shiniest chrome bumpers Peewee had ever seen in his life. Signature plates completed the look with Hillybilly I emblazoned on the fender. There was no question who drove the Ram.

The bumper chrome shone so brightly in the sun that Peewee turned his head away. The polished chrome stood out in sharp contrast to the black primed body of 'The Beast' as Hamn tended to think of the truck.

"Man, I bet you can hear that truck up in Winchester," Peewee said with a smile. Hamn rolled down the window. "What'd you say, Peewee?"

"I said I bet they can hear that truck in Winchester," he hollered over the roar of the engine.

Hamn grinned. "Hope they can. I did put me some black powder in there to make it blow smoke," he confided as he preened in his mirror. His arm tattoos glittered in the sun. "I like loud. Besides, I like to piss off those environmental people. I went out of my way to drive over by JMU."

Peewee's eyes opened. "You drove The Beast by JMU. You're lucky the University police didn't arrest you!"

Hamn spat out the window. "I ain't worried 'bout no pretend University police. But I do like it when those professor dudes shake their fists at me. I just rev it up and blow smoke at 'em." Hamn grinned, obviously pleased with himself.

Peewee nodded. “Cool.”

“They make me sick with all of their ‘do this, do that do this’ rules. It's our earth. We shouldn't have to listen to any of that," he grunted as he jumped out of the truck. Peewee backed up, out of Hamn’s way. He knew better than to be within striking distance of the unpredictable, Hillbilly leader.

Hamn stood in his six-foot five-inch, 300-pound splendor. His bald head shone in the sun. Peewee wondered if he worried about sunburn but decided not to mention it.

"How ya doing?" Peewee asked nervously as he tried to make conversation. He wasn’t comfortable around Hamn. Not now, not ever. Hamn was erratic, volatile, and prone to tantrums. He’d seen him beat the pulp out of guys for no reason at all. Besides, he believed Hamn had most likely killed the guy up at the Mountaineer Conference Center.

Hamn pulled out a red bandanna and mopped his face and bald head. His body was covered in a thin sheen of sweat. His Ray-Ban sunglasses reflected the mountain behind him. Every visible exposed inch of his body was either pierced or tatted. He wore an old leather vest on top of a Motley Crue T-shirt. His jeans were expensive, but his leather boots cost a fortune.

He grinned thinly when he acknowledged Peewee. "What's up, man. Everything under control? You got all the animals we need?"

Peewee nodded and replied in a soft voice. “Yeah. Gonna get a few extra, though.” Peewee’s heart raced. This was the first time he’d been alone with the Hillbilly leader. He didn’t know what to expect.

Hamn nodded. His bald head bounced up-and-down in the sun. He reached for his bandanna and tied it around his shiny head. He stared at Peewee. “I asked you a question. Do we have enough animals?"

Peewee nodded, "Yeah, we got enough,” he said in a loud voice. “But just in case, I'm gonna get a few more traps. I know you don't want to run out of space to put our delivery," he said.

Hamn nodded. He walked towards the cave to inspect the animals. His stride was so long it only took him three steps to reach the outside of the cave. He turned around and looked at Peewee, "Looks good. Get a few more.”

Peewee nodded. “Yeah. I will. No problem,” he said as he shuffled off towards his truck. He looked at Hamn and said, “The old man will be back in a little while. He went to get some Mountain Dew. You gonna be here?”

Hamn nodded “Yeah. I’m stayin’ for a while.”

Peewee was relieved. “I’m takin’ off then.” He decided he’d get a Mountain Dew on the way to pick up a few more animals.

## Chapter 9

"Fancy seeing you again today, Dr. Zimbro," I said as I slid behind Kenzie in line at the Woodstone deli.

Kenzie smiled happily at me. "What are you guys doing here? Where's your sidekick?" she asked as she looked around for LauraLea. "I didn't know you guys ate here."

I shook my head. "We usually don't, but we've been out looking for Gawd Almighty."

Kenzie raised an eyebrow. "Gawd Almighty? Where's Gawd Almighty? Her dark eyes scanned my face, a look of concern in her dark eyes.

I sighed and began my sad saga. "I don't think you know, but he's missing. No one has seen him since yesterday afternoon."

Kenzie's eyes flashed concern. "That's unusual, isn't it? I'm used to seeing Gawd either on the porch or in his cage. What do you think happened?"

I shrugged my shoulders. My heart felt heavy. "I don't know. I just don't know." My voice sounded anxious, so I tried to calm down. "LauraLea and I have looked for him all behind the gallery, down at Rockingham Springs, and up here at Woodstone but no one has seen him."

Kenzie touched my shoulder. "Here comes LauraLea. You gals have time to sit down and eat?"

"Sure, we do," LauraLea answered heartily. "One of the most favorite things Lil and I do is sit down and eat. Right Lily?"

I nodded. "The second thing we love to do is art. Something I'm in vast need of doing," I admitted.

"I grabbed a table over there," Kenzie pointed. "I just got back from Blacksburg. I'm starved to death," she said.

"Did you learn anything?" I was always interested in Kenzie's cases.

Kenzie gave me that knowing look and said, "You bet I did. The plot thickens," she said mysteriously as she handed the waiter a $20 bill. Kenzie grabbed her sandwich and Coke and said, "I'll be over there in the corner."

LauraLea nodded and said, "What do you want to eat, Lily? I'll buy lunch and you can go over and talk to Kenzie. You groove on that frankenfood stuff. I'll just stand in line and stay hot with everyone opening the door and the heat blasting in," LauraLea offered as she gave me her long-suffering look.

I grinned. "Why, thanks LauraLea. You're certainly being nice to me today. I'll take you up on your offer." I knew LauraLea felt bad for me because I was upset about Gawd Almighty but then, so was she. Perhaps, if the opportunity arose, and her husband was working late, I'd treat her to dinner. That's one thing about good friends. They're always good to each other.

I caught up with Kenzie and scooted in close to her at the table. I was dying to know what Kenzie had learned about the Professor and his work at Virginia Tech. She'd flashed me such a mysterious look. I have the greatest respect for Kenzie. She's an excellent forensic pathologist and one of the best physicians I've ever known, and trust me, I've known a lot of them. In addition, she's one of my best friends and always helps me with the forensics in my medical and crime thrillers. Plus, every now and then I get an idea for a book from one of her cases.

"Boy, that smells so good," I said as Kenzie unwrapped her steak sub. “I don't know why but it seems to me like people in this end of the county make the best sub sandwiches anywhere or at least the best steak subs."

"Yeah, they do," Kenzie agreed. "They make the best barbecue too," she added. "Anyway,” she said in a low voice, "I went to Virginia Tech today. Apparently, Professor. Rutledge’s research was top-secret. He had a top-secret security clearance and private and governmental research grants to create the “perfect” genetically modified corn, one that met the safety and growing criteria of American farmers and the concerns of the American public,” she said as she salted her steak sandwich.

“Humph. That’s a tall order. I’m glad no one ever expected me to do anything like that in my research,” I said with a smile

“Me too,” Kenzie agreed. “Anyhow, his research is valued at over $30 million when you consider the eight years he's spent in testing, laboratory testing and so on. Plus, he's received millions in research grants."

I nodded. I was impressed. "This must be some pretty hot corn. And by that, I mean a pretty hot commodity and desired by a bunch of high-powered people."

Kenzie nodded, "Yeah. No question. The FBI is heavily involved. I thought their presence at the crime scene was simply coincidental but now that doesn't seem the case." She gave me a conspiratorial look.

"Yeah, and…" I asked.

"Apparently, there's been problems with folks ripping off genetically modified American foods for years now. It costs US taxpayers billions every year."

My mouth fell open. I had no idea. Why had I not heard of this. I like to think of myself as a reasonably informed person. "Really? I had no idea." I was shocked. I'd never thought of genetically modified corn as a hot commodity.

LauraLea placed our bag of food on the table and then scooted in beside me, "Shut your mouth, literally, Lily. You're either gonna drool, or flies are going to land in your mouth. Which do you prefer?"

“Stop being ugly,” I snapped at Laura and turned back to Kenzie. "I'm shocked. I had no idea," I ignored LauraLea's sarcastic remark.

"What's going on? What are you guys talking about?" LauraLea asked as she unwrapped her sandwich.

“We're talking about people from other countries ripping off America's agricultural secrets. Apparently, Professor. Rutledge had fifty pounds of genetically modified corn worth over a million dollars. Basically, the corn and his research are valued at over thirty million,” Kenzie said as she wiped her hand on a napkin.

LauraLea's mouth fell open, and her pupils dilated in disbelief, just as mine had. I considered being ugly and making a snide comment but decided against it. Sometimes that’s the best decision.

“Thirty million dollars? I can't imagine anyone's research being valued at that much. What is it? The recipe to make gold?" Laura asked, her pupils dilated and the look of disbelief still on her face.

Kenzie laughed. "You'd think so, but it's actually not that exorbitant when you consider a fully staffed lab working ten years to develop a product. I had no idea that Professor Rutledge's work was that highly valued or important. But apparently it is," she said with a grin.

I looked at LauraLea and said, "Apparently, the FBI are involved in this case. Kenzie said they were on the scene today, but she had no idea that they'd be this heavily involved in this case."

"All of this over some genetically modified corn?" LauraLea screwed her face up to show her disbelief. "I can hardly believe someone would care."

"I guess we just have to understand that genetically modified foods are huge business. Remember, we've been growing corn for a long time and it's been hybridized many times over the years," Kenzie reminded us.

"Yep, it sure has, and I think the US is a huge exporter of corn," I agreed.

Kenzie nodded and picked up her sandwich. "One thing I think we don't understand, - not just us, most Americans -is that the number of international economic espionage cases related to theft of American research and technology have escalated from 15% in 2009 to 53% in 2015. A lot of this theft involves our research on genetically modified organisms."

Kenzie stopped to take a bite of her sandwich as I considered what she'd said. I had no idea American agricultural research was under such scrutiny or so vulnerable to attack. In fact, I was amazed to learn this.

"Who's stealing our genetically modified food secrets?" LauraLea asked as scanned her potato chips bag for the ingredients. Laura always said she was cutting down on her salt, but no one cuts down on salt and eats potato chips every day. I shook my head and gave her a dirty look.

“Well, so far we know the Chinese are guilty,” Kenzie said. “Several years ago, three Chinese nationals were charged with stealing high-tech seed corn from several American companies."

"You're kidding. I had no idea that a bunch of corn could be so important," LauraLea said. “Did they convict them?"

Kenzie shook her head and checked her watch. "No, not initially. It was dropped in court due to a technicality."

"How’d they do it, steal the corn?" I asked.

Kenzie shrugged her shoulders and shook her head. "Believe it or not, it was easy - basically a pretty simple operation. The conspirators cruised cornfields in Iowa and Illinois searching for seed company tests fields. Under cover of darkness they stole the seeds and corn. Then they attempted to smuggle the stolen, genetically modified seeds back to their country. They were clever though. They hid the seeds inside boxes of Orville Redenbacher microwaved popcorn."

"Wow, that's amazing. I had no idea. It's so simple it's brilliant," I said as I smiled at Kenzie and shook my head. “How’d they get caught?”

“Someone tipped off the Feds and they apprehended them at the airport. But, you're right, Lily, it was smart and innovative. One of the perpetrators was actually trained in how to develop genetically modified foods." Kenzie shook her head. "I'm still shocked that it was so easy to do."

"So, what are the farmers supposed to do?" LauraLea asked, as her pragmatism surfaced. "Are they supposed to guard their crops with a rifle or put electric fences in?" Laura looked angry. “Farmers can’t do that. They work so hard now...”

I nodded in agreement. "They can't possibly. Farmers grow thousands of acres of crops every year. There’s no way they can grow food and police their farms. It's impossible." I said as I heard a note of righteous indignation climb into my voice. I had a soft spot in my heart for farmers. After all, who worked any harder?

“I agree. You're totally right, Lily. It's a huge issue. All I know that farmers can do, is report strange people and vehicles in the areas of their farm or nearby towns. They must stay alert for strangers. Frankly, that's about it, although it sure doesn’t sound like much."

LauraLea shook her head. "What's this world coming to when people from other countries, and our own country for that matter, steal seeds already planted in the ground? For heaven’s sake, that's just pathetic. It's ludicrous... And dangerous."

“Heck, they even steal them out of the farmer's barn...before he even has a chance to plant them,” Kenzie said in a piqued voice as she picked up her trash and stuffed it in a bag.

I played with the straw in my drink. "How many agricultural genetically modified seed test plots do we have in our area, Kenzie?"

Kenzie rolled the remainder of her sandwich up, squeezed it into a tight little ball. "More than I wanted to know about, especially at Virginia Tech. We have them planted around here as well."

I shook my head. "This could be very, very bad."

Kenzie stood, "You've got that right. Now, it's easier to understand why someone would murder for fifty pounds of corn."

"Yep, a lot easier," I agreed. “Especially since it's worth millions of dollars.”

Kenzie looked down and said, "I've gotta run. I've got a conference call coming in at home." She looked at me and added, “I'll ask

Benson and his guys to look around for Gawd. I'm sure he'll turn up."

I smiled brightly to show my thanks, but I didn't believe Gawd Almighty could get home. If he could, he'd have gone home by now. A sick feeling came over me. I felt flushed.

"See you, Kenzie," LauraLea said. She looked at me and said, "I probably should get back to the gallery." She stared at me. "You okay, Lily? You look a little green."

I assured LauraLea I was fine.

"It's probably getting busy again."

I nodded. "Yeah, I expect it is." Once again, the pain of not finding Gawd Almighty weighed heavy on my heart. I finished my drink, dumped my stuff in the trash can and followed LauraLea.

I opened the restaurant door and the blast of heat took my breath away. LauraLea turned around, "Can you believe all this stuff about the seeds? That's a lot of money for some research." She shook her head and unlocked the car.

I nodded. "It sure is." I looked around Woodstone just once more for Gawd Almighty. “LauraLea, drive around the back near the trash dumpsters. Maybe Gawd got a little hungry,” I said hopefully.

LauraLea dutifully steered her Lexus near the dumpsters but Gawd wasn’t having a late lunch, I’m sorry to report. I got out, looked for him between the dumpsters and called his name. The smell around the area was fetid and rotten in the heat. Even if Gawd Almighty did love snakes and fruit the best, I’m sure he’d never eat anything out of those dumpsters. He’s a class act, an uptown possum.

I returned to the car empty-handed and LauraLea and I drove slowly back to the gallery.

## Chapter 10

The gallery parking lot was full when we returned. LauraLea jumped out and I told her to plan on dinner. My treat. I got into my own car and decided to take a hike up the hill and check on Massanutten's Serenity, my short-term rental home on the mountain.

I'd bought my house up in the Kettle, as they call the area on the mountain where nature scooped out an indention in the mountain shaped like a kettle. The indention can be seen for miles around the mountain. I purchased it several years or so after I returned to Virginia from a long teaching in the school of Nursing at LSU in New Orleans. I'd always planned to retire to my farm in Hanover County, Virginia outside of Richmond. However, I changed my mind because I loved living in the Shenandoah Valley. When I retired from university teaching, I became LauraLea's partner in Artisans Galleries and decided to stay in the Shenandoah Valley. Anyway, I have another home closer to the University in the 'Burg as everyone calls Harrisonburg, Virginia. My Massanutten house has been a short-term rental ever since.

I weaved my way up the mountain and maneuvered the sharp turns carefully. I made a right at Painters Pond and passed the fish truck that had just dumped thousands of fish in the pond for resort guests to catch and hopefully throw back. I continued the drive to my house. I'd seen Gawd Almighty up here several times in the past, so I kept on the lookout for him. There's great things about my house on the mountain, but probably the best thing is the flat driveway. Flat driveways are few and far between in Massanutten and some folks climb an out-and-out cliff to get to and from their homes. A flat drive will increase your property value by a bunch. I've heard thirty percent, but I don't know if that's true. My house looked immaculate on the outside, so I went in and inspected it. Sometimes I forget how much I love the little place, particularly my collection of artwork there. Who knows, maybe someday I'll return there and live. Another great thing about Massanutten's Serenity, the name of the house, is its privacy and lack of yardwork. There's a lot to be said about a natural landscape without worrying about a manicured lawn.

I walked through the house and looked out over the back deck, down to the Golf course below me. My back deck was like a treehouse. In the winter I had a great view of the ski slopes but this time of year the trees covered just about everything. I checked the lower level of the house and everything seemed perfect, even the temperature of the hot tub. I shot a game of pool at my second-hand pool table and returned to the living room. I poured myself a glass of ice water and sat down for a few minutes. I found myself feeling restless, worried, vexed even. Something was bothering me, but I didn't know what it was.

My mind reeled from Kenzie's information about the theft of Professor Rutledge's agricultural research. As I continued to think about her comments, it became clear to me that the theft of technology and research was the motive and reason for Prof. Rutledge's death. But, why murder him? Why not just steal his seeds and research notes? Who'd murdered him and stolen fifty pounds of genetically-modified corn worth several million dollars? I turned the thoughts over and over in my mind until I fell asleep for a few minutes.

I awoke, surprised I'd slept over an hour. I checked my watch and decided to drive up to the highest point of the mountain known as The Lookout. Sometimes I travel there simply for the view or just to think. It's beautiful at The Lookout even this time of year when it's hotter than Hades. I locked my house, got in my Explorer, wound my way back down by Painters Pond headed for the summit. I yielded for oncoming traffic.

I saw that truck again. The same truck, an old green pickup I'd seen yesterday in the gallery parking lot. The truck had a bunch of cages in the back bed. I craned my neck to see if there were any animals in them but, from what I could tell, the cages were empty. I figured the guy must be a hunter or trapper. I really wasn't sure. I followed the pickup and continued towards the top of the mountain to The Lookout.

The road forked, and I turned off towards the The Lookout, but the guy in the green pickup continued up the dirt road. I thought that was strange since the paved road ended and the west fork became an old logging road that lead to the Western slope of the mountain. We'd always been told the only way off Massanutten Mountain during a fire was to take the Western Slope. Fortunately, I'd never been forced to exit that way. My knowledge of the Western Slope was limited. I knew the hiking was good and there were a lot of big animals – mostly bear. I generally stuck to paved roads, even with four-wheel drive.

I sat in my car for about a half an hour, my air conditioning full blast as I considered the facts in Kenzie's case. I hoped the mountain view would offer me some answers, or at least insights, but it didn't look like they were coming today. Plus, a quick trip up the steps to the summit didn't offer my view of Gawd Almighty and that was my primary purpose of the day.

I released my parking break, pulled out of The Lookout lot, and again noticed the road to the Western slope. For a moment I considered driving over there, just to take a ride and see what was there. I wanted to follow the route of the green pickup truck, but my judgment kicked in and I decided that would be an adventure I'd like to share with LauraLea. I checked my watch again and noted it was almost closing time for the gallery. I headed down the mountain, saw her car, and stopped in. I wanted to hit the Western Slope this evening or die trying.

## Chapter 11

Vino greeted me with a happy bark. I noticed his muzzle was stained a little red when I got out of my car, but not nearly as stained as I'd seen it before. Vino seemed to prefer red wine more than white. He licked my hand and followed me onto the gallery porch. For once, the old boy seemed tired, tuckered out which was totally unlike him. Even though he got in trouble for drinking wine, he was in pretty good shape. It seemed an effort for him to walk out in the heat. He gave me a sad, hangdog look, walked ahead and stood in the shade. I was certain he missed Gawd, and I was certain Vino was depressed. The opossum and lab were great buddies. They slept next to each other most nights and played during the day. I filled Vino's water bowl as full as I could and sat on the porch with him for a little bit. I decided to tell LauraLea he needed to stay in the gallery overnight. It was brutally hot. When the last guests finally left the cabin at almost 5:30, Vino had settled down at my feet and was asleep. I disturbed him when I got up and he followed me into the cabin.

I sat at the table, as the air conditioner groaned in pain and blew directly on me. It was like I'd died and gone to heaven. I watched LauraLea as she shut the door after the final customer. She locked it and leaned against it, a sign of relief on her face.

“Busy day,” I cackled from beside the air conditioner.

LauraLea gave me her long-suffering look, her green eyes wide and bright. "Oh, I know I shouldn't say this, but I thought those people would never leave. This is the longest day I’ve spent here in months. I thought these folks would never leave," she moaned. “Sometimes, I don’t think I can do retail. Sometimes I don’t even want to think or be nice,” she snapped as she pushed her perfectly highlighted hair off her forehead with her newly manicured nails.

I shook my head and scratched Vino’s neck. “Really, LauraLea. You’re a pain. You were gone for at least half the day," I reminded her. “How could it be that bad?" I admonished. “You love it every time you fill up the solid gold slushee machine and hear the sound of cha-ching of slushee money in the register.”

She gave me her dreamy look. “Yeah, I like the sound of the Slushee machine and it was a bad day," she scowled as she walked past me to get a glass of wine. "Maybe it’s the heat” she snapped. “Would you like a glass of white wine?"

I shook my head. "No, thanks. I got a Diet Coke.”

LauraLea slipped her flip-flops off and put her bare feet on the heart pine floors. "Oh, even the floors are hot," she complained. "Do you know when we're supposed to get some relief from this heat? It's so oppressive."

I nodded. "Hopefully soon, it can’t last much longer. We know we’ll get a break in September." I took a sip of my Coke and watched LauraLea. She nodded in agreement and walked in the wine room for the bottle of opened blush wine. "

"So, what have you been doing Lily? I thought you were going home and let your dogs out." She refilled her glass.

I lazily checked the color and clarity of the wine and mentally awarded it four points. I used to be a wine judge. Then I picked up the glass and checked for the ‘legs’ on the side of the wine glass.

“Lily, wake up. I’m talking to you,” Laura snapped as she grabbed her glass of wine from me. “Get your own wine if you want a glass,” she spat.

I shook my head. "Oh, I just went up the hill, checked out my house, went up to The Lookout and checked around. No signs of bear.” I paused. “Even though it's hot, it's still gorgeous up on The Lookout."

LauraLea nodded. "I'd imagine it would be. Any signs of Gawd?"

I shook my head. "No, not one. But..." I began.

"But what, what are you thinking?" LauraLea raised her eyebrows as she gave me a sly look. "I know you got something going on in that wretchedly disturbed mind of yours."

I nodded slowly. "I saw something I think we should check out."

"Yeah, what?" LauraLea asked as she got out and brought over the dip and pretzels. "What do you think we should check out."

I paused as I thought about how I should frame the green pickup.

“What. Tell me,” LauraLea said. Patience wasn’t one of her strong assets.

"Do you by any chance remember that beat up green pickup truck that was in the gallery parking lot yesterday? I noticed it fairly early, before lunch, and it was still here when we got back from lunch."

LauraLea squished her face and frowned as she tried to remember. "Are you sure it was yesterday? I remember a funny-looking beat-up pick up the day before that I think was green..."

I shook my head. "Nope, I know it was yesterday. I wasn't here the day before,” I said with assurance. I glared at her when she gave Vino a cracker.

"Nope, then I don't think I saw it. Why?" LauraLea sipped her wine and gave me her full attention. "What do you think?"

"I just saw the truck again. I saw it a little while ago. I was turning on to Resort Drive at Painters Pond. The truck went past me and traveled up towards the Lookout. It was the same green pickup truck. The bed of the truck was full of animal cages.”

LauraLea stared at me. "Animal cages? Why would someone carry animal cages around in the back of their pickup? Were there any animals in them? It's weird to carry animals around August, don't you think?" Laura's green eyes stared into my blue ones.

"Heck Yes, I think!" I said adamantly as I plucked a pretzel from the basket. "I'm convinced it's strange. As a matter-of-fact, it's so strange it's given me a bad feeling," I admitted.

Now I truly had LauraLea's attention. Sometimes she fakes and pretends she's listening. She scrutinized my face. "What are you saying, Lil? Why does it give you a bad feeling?"

I shrugged my shoulders. "I don't know for sure." I paused and took a deep breath. "Anyway, I followed it…him, rather."

LauraLea's mouth fell open. "You followed it?" For heaven sakes, Lily, I told you, don't do that stuff without me." I heard her clamp her teeth together in anger.

I laughed at her. "Don't grit your teeth. I do lots of stuff without you, you know," I said indignantly. Anyway, I followed him up the mountain and I turned to go into The Lookout, but he turned the other way and headed for the Western Slope." I studied LauraLea's face to see if she thought what I did.

"The Western Slope? Why would someone take a pickup truck load full of animal cages to the Western Slope?" She looked confused for second and said, "There's nothing, absolutely nothing over there... At least, that I know of."

"That's right. There's nothing there," I agreed. It's an old logging road. Have you ever been up there?"

LauraLea shook her head. "No, why would I? As you said, there's nothing there."

I held LauraLea's green eyes with my own. I had a flash of insight. "Precisely. Something's going on up there. It's just now come together for me. Do you remember how the ground was pushed down and the grass bent when we searched in the woods yesterday for Gawd Almighty?"

I saw a faint smirk on LauraLea's face. "Yeah. You think whoever was in that green pickup trapped Gawd Almighty, don't you?"

I nodded as my heart rate picked up. "You're darn right I do, LauraLea. I don't know what he's doing with the animals. Probably selling their coats or something disgusting like that," I said as a feeling of nausea overcame me. "We've gotta go get him."

"Get up, we're going up there." LauraLea walked over to the glass knife cabinet and took out two bone-handle hunting knives with six-inch blades. She handed one to me and asked, "Don't cut yourself. Do you have your gun?"

I glared at her as I shook my head. "Nope, I didn't bring it."

"Don't worry about it," LauraLea said as she headed for the back room. "I got an extra one in the safe." She threw the keys at me and said, "Go start the car. It's gonna be hot in there."

I retrieved the keys, left the cabin, and followed LauraLea's instructions. Who was I to buck a woman who was at least seven inches taller than me who had two guns, a knife and a plan to find Gawd Almighty.

I decided to be docile. Totally out of character for me.

## Chapter 12

LauraLea handed me a Glock and a couple of clips. She jumped in her Mazda, a determined look on her face and drove up the mountain. I was glad her daughter had switched out the Mazda for her Lexus this afternoon after she'd delivered wine to the gallery. I had no idea where we'd travel before nightfall and having four-wheel drive was always a comfort to me. The higher we went up on the mountain, the faster my heart pounded.

"Do we have a plan?" I asked as we navigated the hairpin turns at a fair clip. I gripped the leather handrail near the window.

LauraLea flashed me a grin and said, "Nope. No, I don't have a plan. Do you?"

I shook my head. "All I know is someone's planning to do something with those animals and I'm pretty sure it's not gonna be good," I heard the catch my voice and swallowed. I needed to keep it together.

LauraLea's eyes flickered down at my shoes. "How are those for walking shoes?"

“Better than yours, that I’m sure of.” I looked at LauraLea's stylish flip flops and said, "They’re a heck of a lot better than your shoes. That's for sure."

LauraLea shook her head. "I had no idea we were going on pet rescue tonight or I would've worn my running shoes."

I nodded just as a huge, souped-up Dodge Ram truck pulled out right in front of us. The tires on the truck were almost as tall as me. I don't think the guy saw us at all. I whooshed in relief when we weren't sideswiped.

LauraLea hissed one of those non-repeatable words under her breath, screamed at him, and flipped him the bird.

I wanted to slink down and mold myself to the floor of LauraLea's Mazda. I truly expected the guy to turn around, come back and kill us.

"Are you out of your mind, LauraLea?” I gasped. “That guy’s probably gonna turn around and ram us with his big truck." I gulped. “He’ll just knock us over the mountain and no one will find us for years!” My heart beat wildly in my chest. I was freaked.

LauraLea was furious, her face flushed pink. "Let him come, then. I'll shoot him first, trust me," she threatened as her face turned scarlet with anger. “I’ll shoot him more than once – two or three times if I have too.” Her green eyes glistened with anger.

I breathed a sigh of relief as the huge truck continued up the mountain. I glanced over at LauraLea and noticed her breathing had slowed. "You know, it's not out of the realm of possibility that the big dude turns around and shoots us.” I caught a glimpse of myself in the mirror. My face was pale and my eyes dark with fear. “He could still kill us, you know!” I taunted her.

LauraLea glared at me and rolled her eyes. “He’s not coming back. Let it go, Lily. He’ll never turn that monster truck around.”

“Do you really think there's any chance that he isn't loaded with weapons? Did you see the NRA decals plastered on his truck and the rifle rack across the back?" My voice was a bit hostile. “He’s probably running guns or something.” My author brain took off with potential possibilities or what a loaded Dodge Ram truck could do.

LauraLea pressed her finger to her lips. "Let it go, Lily. We're fine. That guy is on his way somewhere he considers pretty important." She slowed her speed to widen the distance between the car and the truck.

We continued to climb the mountain, past Painters Pond and the ski slopes. We passed the Massanutten Conference Center and a few hotels until we came to the fork in the road. LauraLea went left towards the old logging road towards the Western slope.

We drove a couple of miles to the clearing with no difficulty with the road. Then we rounded a steep curve and Laura slammed on the brakes. Both of us shrieked. Directly in front of us, about a hundred yards away, was the notorious black Dodge Ram truck. The truck was complete with double stacks, dually wheels, and the shiniest chrome I'd ever seen. It blinded me, even in the late afternoon sun. For a moment I wondered if he'd painted it with metallic paint. Laura quickly backed into a grove of trees until we were well-hidden from view. Both of us stared at each other white-faced and wide-eyed. LauraLea's white-knuckled fingers clutched the wheel in a death grasp and my finger pressed against the glove box.

My heart sunk and for a moment, I wasn't sure I could catch my breath. It didn't take a rocket scientist to figure out that the guy in the big truck wasn't planning to play nice if he caught us. I stared at LauraLea. Her eyes were bigger than green saucers. I opened my mouth to speak but my voice was a mere croak.

LauraLea flipped the car into reverse and backed her Mazda even further into a thicket of trees. We both sat there and struggled for breath. For a second, I considered calling the Massanutten Police but knew that would be hopeless. No matter which way you sliced the police pie, the Massanutten cops didn't like either one of us. If we called them, we'd both be in the pokey – for trespassing on federal land or driving a vehicle through a bird sanctuary. I'd bet a hundred dollars on that one. I've had an intense dislike with the Massanutten police for some time, but I'll save that story for another time.

LauraLea cut the engine and lay her head on the wheel. I'd never seen her so upset and it kinda scared me. I grabbed her shoulder and shook her. "Sit up, sit up. What's wrong with you. Get your gun out. Suppose the guy comes for us?" I screeched.

LauraLea recovered immediately and reached for her side arm.

I already had my Glock in my lap, safety on.

My brain raced a million miles a minute. *What were we going to tell them if they came over to our vehicle? That we were having an afternoon drive on a logging road? Nope, that wouldn't fly. That we followed a green pickup because he had animal cages? That would get us killed for sure. Perhaps we should tell them we're looking for our pet opossum that had a sleep disorder.* That sounded like the best story to me and I organized it in my mind.

"What are you doing?" LauraLea jeered at me. "I've seen your face change fifteen times in the last thirty seconds. What are you thinking?"

I snarled at her. "I'm thinking up a cover story. Suppose they come over to the car. What do we say?" My voice was a penetrating yelp. It even hurt my ears.

LauraLea's hands still gripped the steering wheel. She looked over at me and I could see paleness below her tan. "Whew, that was close," she admitted. "Let's get out and walk. We'll stay in the woods, out of sight, all right, Lily?"

I rolled my eyes. "Do say, LauraLea. That's a splendid idea," I said sarcastically. "What? Are we going to walk down and see if they need something from the grocery store."?

This time LauraLea rolled her eyes, "Get over it Lily. We have serious work to do here if we're gonna find Gawd Almighty."

I nodded and willed myself to be nice. I took a few deep breaths to calm down my frantically pumping heart. I had to remind myself that even though my spirit was young, and I thought I was young, my heart had a lot of years on it. I opened my door and slid out of the car. It could have been my imagination, but I'm pretty sure the bugs were already out. I was immediately bitten. The air was hot, sticky, and oppressive. "Do you have any of that homemade bug spray in the car?" I'd taught LauraLea how to make bug spray with lemongrass and lavender. It worked well, especially for an essential oil concoction. It even worked in the great state of Mississippi where the bugs were often bigger than your car.

LauraLea nodded, "Look in the glove compartment. There's plenty in there. Do you have your gun?"

I grabbed the bug spray and my purse. I sprayed the air around me. "Yep, let's get walking."

“Is the safety on your gun?” Laura asked.

I didn’t honor that question with a reply.

The two of us walked as quietly as we could through the woods. I kept my eyes peeled for snakes and other unfriendly forest creatures. Within a few minutes, we were both soaking wet with sweat. It was stifling in the woods. It always seemed to me that the hottest part of the day is between five and eight in the evening.

LauraLea put her index finger to her lips and shushed me. I’m not sure why because I wasn’t talking. She whispered, "Do you hear anything. I hear them talking."

I nodded. I did hear conversation. I heard three distinctly different voices.

LauraLea waved me forward. "Let's get closer to see if we can hear," she suggested.

I nodded, and we gingerly picked our way through a bed of pine needles and peered through the pine tree. I felt all kinds of creepy-crawly things move across my feet. I didn't look down, but I shivered inside my skin.

Two men stood beside the Dodge Ram. A third guy, an old man, sat on an old chair. It looked like he was whittling something. The big guy was scary. He was bald with a red bandanna over his head. In my imagination, he was covered with tattoos, but I couldn't see him that well.

"Can you hear anything? Can you make out their conversation?" I murmured to LauraLea.

She shook her head. "Nah. We've gotta get closer. I can't hear what they're saying."

The two of us continued to walk quietly through the woods being careful not to walk on sticks and twigs. We moved closer into a clearing and sat behind a short pine tree.

LauraLea peered through the pine branches and gasped. "No, no. It can't be. There's Ty! The old guy. Remember?" She squinted as she looked again.

"Who is Ty?" I asked. “I’ve never heard you mention anyone by the name of Ty," I said in a hoarse whisper. I was totally confused, and I knew my face showed it.

"Ty, my husband's father's friend...,” Laura said impatiently. “You know, the old guy we saw at lunch yesterday. That's him," she said in a loud whisper.

I looked again. She was right. Despite our precarious situation I smirked at her. "Yep, that. That’s the old guy that gave you the big smacks on your cheeks. Somehow, I don't think he wants to play kissy face with you now," I said in a derisive voice. "What is he, the head of the Hillbilly Gang or something? Isn't that what you told me?"

LauraLea nodded and motioned for me to be quiet. I was, but I couldn't hear anything. "What are they saying?"

"Something about putting the stuff in the cages. I think they said something about moving the animals out, but honestly, I can't be sure." Her green eyes were dark with uncertainty.

My heart leaped with joy. I looked around. “Do you see any animals? I don't." I scanned the area a couple of times.

"They must be holding them someplace else. But, we have no idea where." LauraLea had a despairing look on her face.

I nodded as my hope of finding Gawd Almighty dwindled. Where would these hillbilly goons hide a bunch of animals in cages? It had to be around here because I saw the guy drive the green pickup truck up here.

"What? Where are they going? The three men started to walk. I watched them go about twenty yards beyond the truck and disappear.

LauraLea and I looked at each other. We both were confused. "Where'd they go?"

I shrugged my shoulders. “Beats me.”

LauraLea had tears of frustration her eyes. "I have no idea. But, I'm gonna sit here and until they come back and leave. Then, I'm going over that way and look at where they've been." LauraLea sat down in the pine needles, a determined look on her face, her arms folded into her body.

I sat there and tried to figure out where the three men had disappeared. It couldn't be too far. After all, their vehicles were still close to us. It dawned on me. They'd gone into a cave. That must be it. They had the animals in the cave. I gave LauraLea a triumphant smile. "It's a cave. It must be over there behind those rocks and bushes.

LauraLea smirked and stood up. "You're right, Lily. It must be a cave. The Western Slopes are full of caves and grottoes." Her eyes lit up and her face beamed. "I bet they've got the cages inside the cave. That has to be it." She practically danced a jig in the forest.

I nodded. "Yep it does. We'll just sit here until they leave. I don't care if it's midnight. I promise you, I won't leave this mountain until I'm positive that Gawd Almighty isn't in that cave. Regardless, if there are animals in there, I fully intend to let them out and free them before we get back to your car." I clamped my mouth shut. My jaw was set and there was no way I was going to change my mind.

LauraLea knew I was determined so she didn't argue with me. "Okay, Lily. I just wish I'd known we'd be on a stakeout in the George Washington

National Forest. I'd have bought along a couple of bottles of water and some hardtack," she said with a strained smile.

"We've got water in the car. I'll go back and get it. It doesn't look like anything's gonna change here for a while," I offered.

LauraLea shook her head. "Nah. No need. I'm okay," she assured me. "We'll get the water when we're thirsty. I've got a candy bar in my purse we can split."

My spirits brightened. A candy bar sounded pretty good to me. It'd be a great snack in the middle of the forest while we waited out some dangerous members of the Hillbilly Mob, or gang, or whoever they were. "Okay, get it out and let's split it." I said happily.

There was nothing I loved better than chocolate.

LauraLea reached for her purse and pulled out a giant Hershey bar. She'd handed it to me before we realized the chocolate had melted and was running down LauraLea's arm.

LauraLea grimaced and began to lick the chocolate off her fingers and arm. "Boy, this is a holy mess," she complained. “but it taste’s pretty good.”

I nodded. I could see it was a mess, but I wasn’t about to whine. "Well, at least we’re getting a little energy out of the chocolate bar. I'm gonna lick it off the paper," I announced.

LauraLea and I licked up the chocolate until her hands were clean and my Hershey paper wrapper was pure white. I looked at her as I wiped the sweat off my face and said, "I’d give $50 for a couple of wet ones. I hate being sticky and I'm afraid these bugs will eat us even more since we’re so sweet,” I grinned.

LauraLea scowled at the idea of being bug food. “No question about that. At least we have the bug spray,” she said hopefully.

"Yeah, I hear you. I reached into my purse and pulled out my cell phone. I checked for messages. There were none.

"You better cut that thing off, Lily. One phone call could get us killed," LauraLea said, a serious look on her face. "The Hillbilly Mob, or whatever they call themselves, does bad stuff."

"Obviously," I spat, "they're capturing animals for some sort of bad reason. Of course, they're cruel."

LauraLea flashed me one of her all-time dirty looks and put her finger on her lips. "If you're not quiet, we'll be fish food in Painter's Pond in the morning," she snarled. "Now, button it up."

I shook my head. “Well, it won't take them long to eat us. I saw the fish truck today and they unloaded at least ten thousand fish.”

Laura rolled her eyes.

This had shaped up to be a long night. The last thing I wanted to do was spend the night in the woods in the heat. Being fresh meat for s bear or coyote wasn't part of my life plan. But, I'd do most anything to get Gawd Almighty back and this was the best way I knew to do it.

## Chapter 13

Kenzie pulled her SUV into her driveway at about 7 PM, jumped out of her side and let Solomon out of the back. The black lab jumped down, happy to be free of the car. She'd been at her office in Roanoke most of the day and the traffic on Interstate 81 was bumper-to-bumper due to a wreck.

She opened her front door and collapsed into a chair. She was hot and sweaty from her two-and-a-half-hour drive. Her SUV had never completely cooled off in the bumper-to-bumper traffic. She listened to Solomon in the kitchen slurping large amounts of water from his bowl. She smiled as she listened. She loved that dog.

She stood just as her cell phone rang. It was Benson.

She smiled as she heard his deep voice. She really did enjoy his company, but she wasn't sure she wanted to 'date' him or whatever 30 some year-old widows did with men

"You've had a long day, Kenzie. And I have a cold bottle of Pinot. Shall I bring it over?"

Benson asked. His eyes gleamed at the possibility of seeing the lovely Kenzie.

Kenzie could hear the smile in his voice. "Of course you can." Her heart leapt at the thought of another evening with her lead detective. "Can you give me a half an hour to take a shower? I just walked in."

"Of course, I can. Tell you what, I made seafood kebabs. How about I slip over, put the rice in the steamer, and search out a vegetable. I can also cut the grill on," he suggested.

"Sounds like a plan to me," Kenzie said as her stomach growled. "I haven't eaten since before noon, so I'm starved." She smiled and added, "bring lots of food."

"Done. Anything new on the corn case?"

Kenzie's heart jumped in her chest. "You bet there is! The feds came to see me today and they think the Chinese are behind it, that is, the murder of Dr. Rutledge and the theft of the corn."

Benson paused and whistled, "That makes sense to me. There's seven million people in China who are hungry. Why not steal a few trade secrets from the Americans, and help feed them." Sarcasm was evident in his voice.

"There's more, I'll tell you in a little bit, after I get cleaned up," Kenzie promised.

“See you shortly."

An hour and a half later, Kenzie felt great. Her stomach was full, and several glasses of Pinot Noir had loosened the stress of the day. A slight breeze blew through the woods behind her house. She and Benson sat on her screened back porch. Solomon lay at her feet.

"I saw Lily and LauraLea barreling up the mountain this afternoon," he said with a chuckle. "LauraLea was speeding in her daughter’s Mazda and I mean to tell you she was hitting the gas."

Kenzie rolled her eyes and laughed. "Really. Pedal to the metal, huh. I wonder where they were headed in such a big hurry. It’s interesting that LauraLea would speed. She’s been pretty careful because she knows the Massanutten cops love to give her tickets.”

Benson chucked. “Yeah, they do. They stop her all the time. I remember the last ticket she got.

I can still remember how mad she was. I thought I'd have to get her out of jail."

Kenzie laughed. "Yep. She's lucky the locals didn't arrest her being nasty to them. She was so angry she had smoke coming out of her ears. She fumed about it for months." Kenzie paused. "I wonder where they were headed that was so important," she mused. "I tried to reach them on my way home from Roanoke but neither of them answered."

Benson nodded. "Who knows? I've no idea. They're probably out to eat. You know those two – they're always doing something or going somewhere." He paused and changed the subject. "Anything unusual on the autopsy of Professor Rutledge?"

Kenzie shrugged her shoulders. "No, not really. It's what we expected. Death was instantaneous secondary to the gunshot wound to his head. She scratched Solomon's head, "There was one thing I didn't expect. He had an early onset carcinoma of the lungs. I'm sure it's most likely from working in his lab with pesticides and herbicides. Not that it makes any difference now, but, he had a battle ahead of him with the cancer. That's a tough cancer to beat and the fight would have been a hard one."

Benson shook his head. "Poor Professor Rutledge. All those brains and money and no time to spend it. That's a shame," he lamented. “He probably lived in his lab most of the time like many of them.”

"Yep, he probably did,” Kenzie agreed. "He was, without question, a leading food scientist, and a world scholar in the world of genetically modified organisms. The FBI told me today that he’d already developed a prototype for genetically modified rice that was very successful."

Benson nodded. His dark eyes shone in the light. "That’s certainly impressive. What else did the FBI say? Is his genetically modified rice successful enough to kill for?”

Kenzie reached for her wine. “Possibly. I’m not sure, but people have certainly been killed for a lot less.” She wrinkled her forehead as she often did when she was thinking.

“You said they had more information for you. Did they have any idea someone was after him and his work." Benson settled back in his chair and scooted the foot rest closer to him. It was a beautiful night.

Kenzie nodded. “Yeah. They did. They suspected he was a target and that whoever killed him had had eyes on him for years. Apparently, there are a lot of countries in the world who’d like our knowledge of genetically modified foods.”

Benson nodded. “Yeah, I’m sure. We’re most likely decades ahead of other industrialized countries and third world countries are starving. Plus, with all the natural disasters we’ve had - hurricanes, tsunamis, earthquakes - many areas on the globe have lost their farmland and it’ll take years to reclaim it to the point where you can grow crops again.” He shook his head and reached over to offer Solomon a piece of cheese.

Kenzie considered this and lingered over the thought. “Yeah, and in the meantime, people are literally starving and the price of corn is higher than ever.“ She shook her head. “You’re right, Benson. I’d never considered any of that. The theft of Agricultural intellectual property costs the US billions of dollars every year. The FBI is looking for anyone with any information that helps decrease the theft.”

Benson nodded, his face solemn.

"It's funny," Kenzie said, "I never considered agricultural research as intellectual property. I always think of the biosciences and intellectual theft. You know, like medical treatments and drug research."

Benson nodded "That's a reasonable assumption. Sometimes it's hard for us to get out of our own backyards and see the forest through the trees.

Kenzie's furrowed her brow and played with her long, dark hair. "Apparently, we have, or Virginia Tech has, test plots of genetically modified foods they've planted here. Research test patches, so to speak. A couple of years ago, one of the professors found a doctoral student digging up germinated corn at just after dusk. When the professor confronted him and asked what he planned to do with it, the student acted confused, defensive and secretive." Kenzie looked over at Solomon as he thudded his tail on the floor.

Benson snorted. "It sounds to me like he was stealing plant material. Was he an American?"

Kenzie shook her head. "Nope, he was Korean, North Korean in fact. The University treated it as a crime of intellectual property theft and expelled the student from Virginia Tech."

"Good for them," Benson said. "I applaud that decision. Did they report him to the local police and FBI? We can't have anyone – not American or exchange students, stealing agricultural intellectual property. It's a huge industry, apparently." He cursed softly under his breath.

Kenzie nodded. "And expensive. No argument here. They also told me about a young research assistant in the Midwest who stole plant material and passed it on to friends. He had a suitcase full of germinated plants and corn seeds at the airport – and that's just a few of the most recent attempts to steal agricultural property," she said as she pressed her lips together in annoyance. "It's apparently pervasive. People want our agricultural intellectual research, no question about it."

Benson shook his head. "I don't doubt it. America has always had the best research in many areas. I can't imagine being a farmer, working myself to death in the fields every day, and have someone dig up my crops or steal seed from my barn," he said as he clasped his hands behind his head and leaned back in his chair. "This is serious stuff."

“Yep. It’s big time. I’d feel the same about any intellectual property, any health sciences research, biosciences, agricultural research, weapons, anything," Kenzie said as she stood and opened the porch door to let Solomon out.

"Was there anything else the FBI noted? Not that that's not bad enough," Benson asked.

Kenzie watched Solomon water the trees in the woods behind her house. She returned to her seat and leaned her head against her lounge chair and fluffed her hair. "Yeah. It seems we have a couple of test acres planted here, in Rockingham County. We have several variations of the genetically modified corn that are being tested here. As a matter of fact, a tour of these test acres was part of Professor Rutledge’s presentation this week. The Rockingham Sheriff's office reported to the FBI that those test plots had been disturbed – disturbed in that someone had dug up some six to eight-inch seedlings this past spring."

Benson whistled. "The plot thickens. Any idea who did that?"

Kenzie shook her head. "Nah. The Sheriff’s office blew it off until this other stuff happened with

Professor Rutledge a couple of days ago. Initially, they thought it was just kids. Hang on..." She paused as her phone signaled a text. It was from Lily. "Oh, good. Lily thinks they may have found Gawd Almighty. He's been missing for almost two days."

Benson nodded "Yeah, I heard that this afternoon when I stopped at the gallery and bought the wine. Where'd they find him?"

"On the Western Slope, of all places. Why would Gawd Almighty go up to the Western slope? Kenzie questioned. "Why would he even leave the gallery? He has it made in the shade there. People feed him all the time and he has a soft bed in his crate," she giggled.

"Yeah," Benson agreed. "Plus, he has Vino for company. They are bed-fellows most of the time."

Kenzie nodded. "Yeah, they are. They sleep together and they're great friends. Sometimes, I think Solomon feels a little left out," she admitted as she glanced outside at her dog.

Benson smiled. Kenzie could see his entire face light up. "Solomon can handle it. He's a tough old boy."

Solomon heard his name and appeared at the back door and whined to get in. Benson opened the screen door and the big black lab lay on the porch and panted heavily.

“It’s still hot out there,” Kenzie noted, “or he wouldn’t be breathing so heavily.”

“Yeah. It is. But, getting back to Lily and Laura, a better question would be why would anyone go to the Western Slope? There's nothing up there. It's just an old road,"

Kenzie nodded. A flicker of concern crossed her face. "You don't think they're up there now, do you?"

Benson shook his head. "I certainly wouldn't think so. At least, I hope not. There's lots of bears and other unmentionable big beasts... and small creatures...up there that are out this time of year. It's desolate up there." He paused, “If they’re up there, they could easily get in trouble.”

Kenzie's mind raced. "Certainly, they wouldn’t be up there now, it's turned dark."

"Yup, it has. And I just felt my first mosquito bite." Benson stood and he, Kenzie and Solomon filed into the house. Benson didn't tolerate mosquitoes at all

## Chapter 14

The sunlight faded, and the forest became dark and quiet. I looked over at LauraLea. She'd rested her head and upper body against a tree. Her eyes were closed.

I nudged her foot with mine. "Well, what do you think? We've been sitting up here for about two and a half hours. I'd have thought a couple of those guys would've left by now. Wouldn't you think?" I said with an impatient toss of my head.

LauraLea's eyes popped open. "Yeah! I certainly would've thought so. I'm not looking forward to spending the night with you in the woods," she laughed.

"What did you tell your husband? Did you let on that his Daddy's friend had captured helpless animals illegally?"

LauraLea shook her head as she scratched her foot with her other foot. "Nah. No, no need for that until I can tell him in person." She hesitated, "Look, look Lily. It looks like one of them... wait, maybe two of them are leaving."

I stood and peered through the bushes. Sure enough, the great big guy with a bald head and red bandanna walked towards his ginormous Dodge Ram. He jumped in, fired up his Cummins diesel, and gunned his motor. I was shocked at the black smoke that blew out of the stacks behind the cab. In fact, it made me mad.

“Will you look at that? Holy crap. Somebody should arrest him for air pollution. That's the nastiest fuel emission I've ever seen." I was incensed, enraged as I shook my fist at the monster truck.

LauraLea stood with her hand over her mouth she was so stunned. She had a sour expression on her face. I saw her blow air out her cheeks, something she often did when she was irate or furious about something. She shook her head and compressed her lips. "I got a good mind to call the Massanutten police and have them pick him up at the guard house! I hate people who pollute the environment like this."

"Do you think those things, that engine or whatever it is, is legal? I don't see how they could be." I grimaced as the guy gunned his engine a couple more times. I was certain any forest animals who were close by had run toward the biggest hill they could find. I hated the feeling of powerlessness that overcame me when I experienced stuff I couldn't fix.

I watched him back up the beast truck as I scratched the top of my foot. I wished I had some of that bad-for-you bug-spray... the one with all the chemicals in it. I had a feeling my body was gonna be a mass of whelps and bites by the time I got home. For a moment, I longed for my home. I'd be all nice and snug, inside with my dogs with no bugs bothering me. Plus, it'd be cool and that would be nice.

"Look at that son of a gun," LauraLea hissed. He's leaving the mountain. He's goin' down the Western Slope. I didn't know there was a road." She stared at me, her eyes dark pools in the lowlight.

I shook my head. "Well, I guess when you're driving a barge with a million horsepower and humongous wheels you can get most anywhere."

LauraLea watched the man but remained silent. I knew she was angry. She was worse at powerlessness than me. We both watched the huge truck descend the Western side of the mountain until it disappeared.

I shook my head and said, "Well, one down. At least the odds are more in our favor." I was delighted the big guy had exited-black smoke and all. Now, if Mr. Green Pickup would take off, I'd take my chances. I figured I was pretty well matched with the old guy."

LauraLea read my mind. "If that other guy would leave, I'd go down there and search for the cave. Should we plan on that?"

I nodded. "Yeah, I'm fairly sure we can take on grandpa. He's probably armed, but, we do have a couple of guns," I said with more bravado than I felt. The guy was a creep and I didn't feel like tussling with him, but...

"We have two hunting knives, too. Yeah, that old dude won't be any trouble." LauraLea looked me up and down., "You can probably outrun him, Lily. He's a pretty old geezer."

"Yeah, I probably can," I said after some consideration. "I wouldn't dismiss him lightly though. You're the one that said he was the leader of the Hillbilly Mob. He probably has a lot of fight left in him plus he looks like a nasty critter."

“Probably does and he is a nasty old coot. At any rate, we're not gonna fight because we're gonna waltz in there and take him by surprise. I'll hold the gun on him while you look for Gawd Almighty. Sound good?" LauraLea’s voice was confident.

I stared at her. "Are you off your rocker? We’re not gonna waltz anywhere. Let's just hope green truck leaves soon. I'm hungry," I announced. As usual, my mood was governed by the state of hunger and I could feel grumpiness setting in.

LauraLea rolled her eyes. "We’re always hungry. Both of us are, but that’s not new. But both of us have enough stored fat to get us through the battle."

I gave her my grumpy look. I wasn't a nice person when my blood sugar dropped. In fact, I could be downright mean. I decided I didn't want to start with a war of words tonight. “I'll just grit my teeth and get through."

LauraLea didn’t reply. She watched the clearing where the vehicles were parked. I figured the old Chevrolet was the old guy’s vehicle.

I looked up and noticed the moon was almost full. I elbowed LauraLea. "Uh oh. Check out the moon. You know that when the moon is full all kinds of crazy people are out."

LauraLea laughed. "We are out, so I guess that's true."

"I'm not worried about us. It's those Hillbilly Mob people that I think are crazy, mean and ugly," I said defiantly.

"Look, look." LauraLea pointed her finger. It looks like Mr. Green Pickup is leaving," she said excitedly as she wagged her finger and pointed at him.

Sure enough, the guy came into view with no cages in his hands. He ambled over to his beat up green truck and got in."

LauraLea's eyes followed his movements. "You wanna guess which side of the mountain he departs?"

I shrugged my shoulders. "I've got no idea. I know what side he came up. He traveled up the Eastern slope, through the resort. I guess that's the way he'll leave too."

"Yeah. Probably will. I don't think the police are gonna chase him based on his beat-up pickup."

LauraLea and I watched until the green truck picked up speed and headed toward Resort Drive. We watched until the vehicle was out of sight.

"Are you ready?" LauraLea gave me a long, shrewd look.

I nodded but panic encased me for a second. "I'm as ready as I'll ever be, so let's do it. By the way, how much battery do you have on your cell?"

LauraLea checked her phone. "About half. You?" she asked as she studied the moon.

“About the same. Let's try to find the cave without using a flashlight. I don't wanna alert grandpa that we’re on the way."

"Good plan. Let's do it," LauraLea said with more bravado than she felt. Later I planned to tell her I didn't need the cheerleader jolt, but perhaps she did.

The two of us walked quietly through the woods in the direction of the area where the men had disappeared and later emerged. The moonlight on the forest floor made navigation easy.

We walked around the bushes and rock and were immediately enveloped in total darkness. "What the heck happened to the moon?" LauraLea whispered, a frantic note in her voice."

"It's behind the cloud," I whispered. “By the way, keep your voice down. Grandpa may not have lost his hearing yet."

We walked about fifteen more feet in the darkness. LauraLea searched the sky. "That moon needs to move out of the clouds. I can't see a stinkin’ thing," she whispered

"You should be able to see better than me. You're a lot younger," I whispered in my grumpy voice. As scared as I was, my stomach was starved and making noise.

LauraLea cut on her phone flashlight for second. Directly in front of us was a large rock opening that could easily be the entrance to a cave.

My left hand shot up to my mouth and I pointed. LauraLea nodded and quickly turned the flashlight off. It fell to the ground and we spent the next ten minutes barefoot trying to find it in the darkness.

I heard a strange noise. I think it was an animal, maybe a coyote. I stood there paralyzed in fright, unable to move. *What were we doing? We were two women in the middle of the George Washington Forest at night. What's worse is we plan to enter a cave that was darker than Dante's hell.* I stood there and took a few breaths. I looked over at LauraLea. I could tell she'd hesitated as well.

"I think that sound was a bird," she said.

"A bird? A bird my foot, LauraLea. It was something wild," I hissed. "Something that most likely wanted a piece of us for a snack."

LauraLea was defiant. The moon came out and I could see the cheeky look in her eyes. "It was a bird. I know it was a bird," she insisted angrily. She stared at me. "What? Are you scared? Should we rethink this?" LauraLea squinted at me in the moonlight. I could see hesitation in her eyes.

I gave LauraLea my favorite 'are you out of your mind look' and turned my head away. In truth, we were both out of our minds.

Chapter 15

I reached for her arm. “Nope. We can do this, LauraLea. We’ve got to find Gawd Almighty.”

“I know,” she said sullenly. “We *can* do this. We’re smart and well-armed.”

“That we are,” I agreed.

Both of us nodded in affirmation, removed our guns from their holsters, held them in front of us like they did on TV, and walked into the cave. I hesitated for one second and sent a text message.

It was black as pitch in the cave. LauraLea beamed her flashlight around the sides of the cave. Sure enough, there were twenty-five or thirty cages of animals. Most of them were quiet. Every now and then, one of them would make a sound that echoed in the cave and gave me chill bumps. My heart raced. I figured that any lumps of cholesterol that blocked my blood vessels would be dispersed tonight. Hopefully, I’d live through it.

"You see any sign of grandpa?" I asked LauraLea.

She shook her head. "I searched up and down the sides of the cave but didn't see any humans. Only animals. "Maybe he's in a sleeping bag somewhere. Or maybe there's a way out the back or side of the cave."

I shuddered. "Yeah. Maybe there is a way out." I knew I didn't want to be in here all night. I was already cold and clammy.

LauraLea seemed annoyed and sighed deeply. "The old guy's most likely here. He's got to be around here somewhere." Her voice sounded frustrated.

I watched her take two steps forward. I could tell she was beside the first row of animal cages.

I was stunned. "What's all of that light on the floor and in the cages?" I asked, awed and a little frightened by the sight. The animal cages had small lighted areas that gleamed in the darkness like diamonds or rhinestones."

LauraLea shook her head. "I don't know. But it's weird. It looks like lights… kinda like the cages are decorated or something. What in the heck is going on?" I felt her body shudder next to me. It occurred to me that we clung to each other at that moment.

She took a couple more steps to inspect the other rows of cages. "It looks the same back here. Every cage seems to have lights. Some have more than others."

I moved behind her. The lights were strange, kind of eerie, creepy even. I had no idea what the source of the light was. I wasn't about to stick my hand in a cage because for all I knew, the animals were rabid and would bite my finger off. *My momma didn't raise any dummies.* I needed all my fingers for my computer keyboard.

Then I heard a loud sound, a burst of air and a cry from LauraLea. The cave went pitch black. It was so dark I couldn't see my own finger in front of my face. I quickly switched on my flashlight and moved towards the sound. My heart wanted to jump out of my chest.

"LauraLea, LauraLea, where are you?" My voice sounded frightened and pathetic as it echoed through the cave. I was frantic with fear and concern.

No response. I moved a step closer and called again.

"Darn it, LauraLea. Where are you." My gun was in the ready position in front of me. I took another step and shined my light toward the floor of the cave. I heard a strangled sob. I moved my light up and found LauraLea. Grandpa had her. He leaned against a big rock with LauraLea in front of him. His forearm was around her neck. LauraLea's eyes were dazed with fear and pain.

Panic and dread shot through my brain. "Let her go. Let her go right now," I ordered, "or I'll shoot you," I threatened. I steadied my left 'gun' hand with my right so he couldn't see my hand tremble.

The old man let out a raunchy, coarse laugh and said. "No way. I've been wantin' this here lady for long time." The old man gawked at Laura. I saw the way he looked at her and my skin crawled. I knew she'd scratch his eyes out if she saw the look of lust on his face. In fact, given a chance, Laura would probably beat him to a pulp.

The hillbilly mob member disgusted me. His beard was dirty, still nasty with pizza sauce from a few days ago. I could smell his unwashed body. The low light in the cave gave him a menacing and sinister look. For a moment, I mentally willed LauraLea to pull his beard and cause him tremendous pain. Unfortunately, the wily, cunning old man had pinned one arm under her body and her other arm was wedged between her body and the side of the cave. She didn't have access to either of her arms. He'd also placed one of his legs over LauraLea and she couldn't move them. I watched her struggle against him.

The old man grinned at me. He was evil, crafty and sly.

I was mad. My voice was strong. "I swear, I'll shoot you. Let her go! I switched my flashlight off, switched my phone on and dialed 911. I prayed silently. Maybe, just maybe, the Massanutten police could help in this dire situation. I switched my flashlight on and shined my light directly in the old geezer's eyes. I temporarily blinded him. I typed in 'Western Slope'.

"I guess you'll have to shoot then," the man rasped and coughed. I wondered how many cigarettes he'd smoked to get that voice and the cough. He reached up his other hand and showed me a wooden handled boning knife. It looked sharp.

"If you shoot me, then I'll use my knife on her. Is that what you want, little lady?"

LauraLea's eyes were huge with fear at her mouth was open. I saw her try to wiggle her way down his body, but he jerked her back up to where she'd been. He pressed tighter against her neck. I knew he had cut off part of her air supply.

I saw LauraLea smile. I knew she was trying to tell me something. I didn't know what.

I stood there motionless, as I stared into the old man's eyes. I decided to talk to him to buy some time.

"Aren't you good friends with LauraLea's father-in-law? How do you think he's gonna feel when he finds out you've hurt his daughter-in-law, the mother of his grandchildren?" I asked in an accusing tone. I shined my light directly in his eyes again, the only way I had to show my anger.

He put his hand over his eyes and said in a rough voice. "You shine that light in my eyes again and I'm gonna kill her just for the heck of it," he threatened.

I moved my light against the wall for a couple of seconds and then cut it off. We were in complete blackness. For the life of me, I had no idea how much time had gone by since we'd been in the cave. My thoughts were interrupted by his hateful, raspy voice.

"Come on, little lady," he cajoled in his gruff voice. "Throw your gun over to the other side of the cave and I'll let you and LauraLea walk out of here."

I laughed. "Do you expect me to believe that? I must look like a total moron to you." My voice was indignant but I was scared beyond death.

I felt him laugh at me in the dark. "Nope, you look like a lady 'bout to get herself in serious trouble," he said hoarsely. I could see his rotting teeth in the beam of my light.

I took a moment to pull out my knife. Heck, what did I have to lose? I might as well use both of my weapons on him if I could get LauraLea away from him. I contemplated pitching my knife at him. I'd taken a knife tossing course a few years ago. I'd been pretty good at it. I was also still very good at darts. But I didn't know if I could hit him. LauraLea's body covered most of his. As I considered my options, I realized the old man had been sitting behind a boulder when LauraLea walked by. My guess was he pulled her foot out from under her and she'd fallen on him. *What a nasty creep.*

"I told you, lady. Throw your gun across the cave or it's gonna be curtains for your friend," the man snarled at me. I could tell her was short on patience. I caught a whiff or his rancid breath.

I beamed my light against the cave wall and I could see the evil and malice in his eyes. I knew he was serious.

I took a deep breath and said, "Okay, you win. But tell me, what are those diamond-like things in the animal cages? I have no clue what they are."

A harsh laugh rumbled up from the old man's chest and out of his mouth. "Them's diamonds ain't nothing but corn. Some corn, a special corn we're gonna sell to somebody for an awful lot of money, millions of dollars, maybe." he gloated.

My jaw dropped. I couldn't believe it. Was it possible these men had stolen the corn and murdered Professor Rutledge? I'd expected nothing like that. I'd just come up here looking for my possum with a sleep disorder. I knew I needed more time to think. I had to buy some more time.

"Corn? Do you expect me to believe that?" I scoffed at him. "Corn doesn't glow-in-the-dark or look like diamonds," I insisted in my most haughty voice. "You're lying. I think you've stolen diamonds or something."

The man rolled his filthy head back-and-forth on the tall boulder he leaned against. He held LauraLea in a firm grip. "It's corn, I tell you. But it's as valuable as diamonds," he said with a harsh, raspy laugh.

"Of course, it is," I said in the most sarcastic, sickly-sweet voice I could muster. "Corn always looks like diamonds, doesn't it, LauraLea," I said with a laugh

I heard a muffled sound come from LauraLea's throat, but it was nothing I could understand.

The man reached behind the boulder he lay against and pulled out a burlap bag that glittered like thousands of diamonds in the dark. He reached his hand into the bag and threw a handful of corn at me. His forearm remained pressed against LauraLea's windpipe. At that second, I thought I heard the purr of an engine headed towards us.

Keeping my gun level, I reached down and picked up a couple of the florescent, twinkling kernels. Sure enough, it was corn. I looked into LauraLea's eyes, but I couldn't see her much. She looked less frightened. Her eyes blinked as she looked toward the cave entrance.

"Are you satisfied, little lady?" Perhaps you'd like to come closer and take a better peek?"

"Where'd you get the diamond corn?" I surprised myself with the question. I'd run out of conversation and figured I was about out of time. I prayed someone would come and help us.

The old man laughed. "I may be old but I ain't dumb and one thing I don't do is tell names and tales both."

I strained my ears in hopes I'd hear signs of help but all I heard was the hum of nighttime insects. "I asked you," I said loudly, "where'd you get the corn? Nobody here makes golden corn," I said as I shone my light and moved a little closer to LauraLea.

The old guy was getting belligerent. He snarled at me. "I told you. I ain't telling. Now you get yourself over here or I'm gonna kill your friend."

At that second the cave came alive with light. I heard voices outside. Grandpa turned his head towards the mouth of the cave. As he struggled to sit up and see where the light came from, I clipped off a shot and hit him in the elbow. He yelped in pain as LauraLea bit his forearm and jumped away from him. She staggered and almost fell but I was able to extend my arm to break her fall. I grinned at her. "I hope you don't have rabies," I joked. "I'd have never bitten that nasty old man," I assured her.

A second later Kenzie stood with us and helped LauraLea and me safely out of the cave. Benson had already handcuffed grandpa who'd already spilled his guts about the Hillbilly Mob.

Kenzie looked at the two of us and said angrily, "You guys have got to be out of your minds. What were you thinking?" Her face was marked with rage and irritation at the same time. Or, perhaps I misread it. Maybe it was relief.

“We were looking for Gawd Almighty,” I said stubbornly. “We think he’s locked up in one of those cages in there.”

Kenzie nodded. “I’ve seen the old man around the mountain. He’s bad, mean. The game warden knows him well. I've seen him around the mountain with animal cages. He would've killed both of you." She gazed at LauraLea, "You're lucky you're alive. Why didn't you call us for help at six o’ clock?"

I now read anxiety and distress on Kenzie's face. "Honestly, Kenzie. It happened so fast. I put together the green pickup truck that was loaded with animal cages and a bunch of tampered grass and shrubs we saw in the woods behind the gallery. It added up to Gawd being taken.

"Okay," Kenzie agreed. "But you all were up here by yourselves in the George Washington National Forest after dark with known criminals a matter of yards from you. You can't tell me you believe that was good judgment," she said, her voice bordered on anger. I knew she was frustrated. I knew she considered us her adopted mothers.

I hung my head. I hadn't felt this ashamed in years. I looked over at LauraLea who hadn't spoken and pointed at her. "She made me do it. It's LauraLea's fault," I said with a short giggle. It was the only way I knew to diffuse the situation... and our abject stupidity.

I felt LauraLea's body stiffen beside me. "Are you out of your mind, Lily. It was both of our ideas to come up here. We wanted to find Gawd Almighty and...."

"Lily, LauraLea, you ladies come back in here. Be careful, though, the floor is uneven." Benson motioned to us and added, "Kenzie, you come too. I want you to see this," he said, a wide grin on his face.

The three of us traipsed very carefully back to the furthest row of cages. We walked between two rows to where Benson had squatted. Most of the animals were sleeping or had retracted into their skin from either fear or the light. A few of them made scared, whimpering sounds.

Benson smiled from ear-to-ear. "Lily, look, look over here," he said, his handsome face reflected in the lighting.

I bent down and peered into the cage. There was my beloved Gawd Almighty. LauraLea and I both gave a screech of excitement and hugged each other. “We found him, we found our poor opossum. Gawd Almighty looked up at us, his eyes open, even though it was night. I briefly wondered if his sleep disorder was healed. I sort of hoped not because if he slept during the day, we’d never see him.

I turned my face as tears streamed down my cheeks. I was so thankful that we'd survived and found Gawd. Life couldn’t be better at this moment.

"Oh, I'm so thankful", I said as I turned around. I smiled at Kenzie and Benson. "Thanks for saving our tails and Gawd Almighty," I said simply. “I love you guys,” I added as I hugged the two of them.

LauraLea echoed her thanks and hugged Kenzie and Benson as well. "You guys are the best friends the two of us could ever have," she says as tears fell down her cheeks.

“Yeah,” I said. “Dumb and dumber. That’s us!”

Benson laughed and said, “Now, Lily. We didn’t say that. You did.”

Kenzie beamed back at us, "Thank you for finding Professor Rutledge's killer and millions of dollars of genetically modified corn."

My hand flew to my mouth in surprise. I hadn't put together the fact the corn we found was *the* corn. I was so excited I could hardly speak, "Oh, that's the corn?" I asked stupidly.

Kenzie nodded happily. "It's shiny because it has a biodegradable marker, so it can easily be identified and/or picked out or isolated from other corn. That's why it glows in the dark," she explained.

LauraLea looked around the cave and asked, "Where is the corn. All I see is a half a bag of it."

"It's right here," Benson said. "This is pretty clever." He pulled out the bottom of each animal cage and showed us another false bottom in the cage that held approximately two pounds of genetically modified corn. "They'd planned to sneak the corn off the mountain to who knows where, in these animal cages." Benson paused a moment and added, "Pretty smart for a bunch of hillbillies."

I was dumbfounded by the discovery. LauraLea shook her head and was for once, speechless.

Benson looked at Kenzie and said, "Ingenious for the Hillbilly Mob, isn't it," he said with a thin smile.

"Not that smart," Kenzie said. "We won. We got back the corn, Gawd Almighty, and we found Professor Rutledge's murderer! It's a good night... all and all," she said as she stared at LauraLea and me. "And, Lily and Laura live to fight another day," she laughed.

"I suppose you're right," he said as his face crinkled up and his laugh lines became visible in the light. He beamed at LauraLea and me, "Let me get you ladies out of here. It's chilly in here and it can't be good for any of us."

LauraLea opened her mouth, "But... But," she said as her voice trailed off. "What about..."

Benson put his arm around her and said, "He's on his way now. There's an officer who has placed Gawd Almighty in my truck and will take him down with you and Lily and put him in his cage or kennel or whatever it is."

"It's his bed," I snapped, my grumpy mood back because I realized I was hungry. I decided to adjust my attitude. I'd been hungry before.

LauraLea smiled gratefully at Benson.

We walked out of the cave and I felt appreciative for everything that had happened. I was happy when the blast of summer hot air blew in my face. I hoped I never visited another cave. I hoped I wouldn't die from a mosquito bite infection. Most of all, I was thankful for friends.

Once again, life was great on Massanutten Mountain.

****The End****

***Please enjoy my own personal favorite Corn Chowder Recipe on the last page of this book!***

Dear Readers,

Thank you so much for reading *The Most Awfullest Crime of the Year: Gawd Almighty and the Corn*, my second Artzy Chicks cozy mystery. If you liked the book, it would mean a lot to me if you leave me a review on Amazon.

I would love for you to join my no spam mailing list where I offer great discounts on my books and the books of other terrific authors I recommend. To join my list and receive a free book, visit www.judithlucci.com/. I love to hear from my readers. Feel free to contact me via my website or email me at judithlucciwrites@gmail.com.

RECIPE

Guys, many of you know I used to own a Virginia Farm Winery. We used to have barrel tastings of our new vintages during the winter months. So... we'd host White Wine and Corn Chowder on our soup weekends. Here's a terrific recipe. Often times I quadruple it...freeze some for later.

**Windy River Corn Chowder Almighty**

**Ingredients**

(Serves 6)

- 1 ½ lbs. of frozen corn (fresh corn appx. 4 ears)
- 1 tsp butter
- 8 oz bacon
- 2 tbsp
- 1 garlic clove
- 1 small onion
- 5 tbsp
- 2 cups chicken broth
- 3 cups milk
- 1.2 lb potatoes cubed
- 2 sprigs of thyme OR 1 tsp dried thyme
- 3/4 cup cream
- 3/4 cup scallions
- Salt and finely ground pepper to taste

Judith Lucci

## Directions

1. If using fresh cut the corn off the cob. This is how I do it: Place a small ramekin in a large bowl. Place corn on the ramekin then cut the corn off. See video. Keep naked cobs.
2. Place 1 tsp butter in a large pot over medium high heat. Add bacon and cook until golden. Use a slotted spoon to remove onto a paper towel lined plate. Leave fat in pot.
3. Lower heat to medium high. Add 2 tbsp butter, once melted, add garlic and onion. Cook for 2 - 3 minutes until onion is translucent.
4. Add flour and mix it in. Cook, stirring, for 1 minute.
5. Add broth, milk, potatoes, thyme and bay leaf. Break naked cobs into 2 or 3 and add into the liquid. Put the lid on and simmer for 25 minutes (adjust heat so it's simmering energetically but not bubbling like crazy or super gently).
6. Remove lid, remove corn cobs. Add corn and cook for 5 minutes or until cooked to your taste.
7. Stir through cream and 3/4 of the bacon and shallots. Adjust salt and pepper to taste. Ladle into bowls and garnish with remaining bacon scallions.

I use heavy / thickened cream. Feel free to use half and half, pouring or even light cream. Butter is also a great option if you don't have cream - just a small bit to add richness. Sometimes, I add chicken if I have left over chicken. It just makes it even better.

Enjoy!

## The Most Glittery Crime of the Year:

## The Jewel Heist(Book 3 of The Artzy Chicks Mysteries)

### Chapter 1

I usually don't get to the Artisans Gallery early in the morning, or anywhere early for that matter. I figure that's my reward since I've passed the half-century mark. However, it was my day to "mind" the store, otherwise known as the Artisans Gallery, a unique gallery of incredible art created by Shenandoah Valley artists. Collectively, our artists are known as "The Artzy Chicks" and while we're all uniquely talented, several of us bring the words ditzy and zany to life. The gallery is housed in a 1700s log hunting cabin in Arboretum Park at Massanutten Resort. The cabin has been added on to and renovated several times, mainly around 1800. The gallery is busy during the spring and summer when the mountain laurel blooms and the kids are out of school. In the fall, the leaf-peepers converge on us like a swarm of locusts. In the winter, we get the ski folks and snow sports enthusiasts. We've found they're not as likely to buy art, but they love to taste wine and drink wine Slushees.

We're also home to a menagerie of animals. We have Gawd Almighty, the possum that was kidnapped a while back, Vino, our yellow lab, and Rembrandt, our calico cat who's tasked to keep the mice down and the snakes under control. Also, Solomon, medical examiner Kenzie Zimbro's black lab is often part of our animal mix.

Vino greeted me with a slow wag of his tail. He stretched his long, golden body in the summer sun and watched as I approached. He knows the sound of my vehicle. He's a good ole boy who just appeared at the gallery one day. Life here is good for him and he's never disappeared, except for when I take him home to live with me in the winter. We're only open part-time after Christmas because we don't have central heat, and I can assure you it's freezing in that log cabin. The wind chill factor is below zero when the breeze rushes through those hand-hewn logs. When we're open, we huddle around a gas stove and a few electric heaters, and drink endless cups of tea, coffee, or whatever's handy which oftentimes includes mulled wine.

The Artzy Chicks love animals. We each have four or five of our own, and we take turns caring for the gallery's pets. I'm in charge of Vino's vet bills, but so far, he's been healthy which is good because he does have a few vices.

Vino, along with Gawd Almighty, generally hang out on the porch and greet people. Vino ran over to greet me. I reached down, patted his head, and frowned at the pieces of cork in his teeth. His muzzle was stained a dark shade of purple. I groaned to myself. Vino's a drinking dog, a wino canine meaning that he just flat out loves to drink. Every time I take him to the vet, I expect to hear he has pancreatitis or poor liver function, but so far, we've been lucky. I shook my head and wagged my finger in his face. He hung his head. He knew I was gonna fuss at him. In fact, I was gonna bless him out.

"Vino, you've been bad. You've been in the wine again, and I bet you've eaten the corks in the barrel LauraLea was saving for the cork wreath-making class, haven't you?" I scolded. "She's gonna be so mad!"

Vino laid his head on his paws and looked away from me. I walked around the back of the cabin, and sure enough, Vino, or some other wild critter from the George Washington Forest, had turned over the barrel of wine corks. Hundreds of corks lay on the ground. I made a face at the lab who watched me carefully from a safe distance. I picked up corks for ten minutes. I threw the badly chewed corks away and salvaged the ones I could. I made a mental note to tell LauraLea, the Diva, to move them into our tiny storage area; that is, if she wanted a wreath class before the holidays.

Oh, before I go any further, let me introduce myself. I'm Lily Lucci. I'm mostly a writer of crime, mystery, and thrillers, but I'm also a watercolor artist and silk painter. I'm also an almost fully retired professor of nursing at a major university. Just today, LauraLea asked me if I'd teach an acrylic painting class. Yuck. Can't wait. That's being ugly, and I realize that. For me, touching the brush on the paper with watercolor creates a lovely, magical painting, but filling a brush with heavy acrylic paint and applying it to canvas is hard work. But it's all great fun. Plus, I love to teach folks to appreciate art and colors. I truly believe that anyone can paint. If you just do it over and over, you'll become a good artist.

I walked around to the front of the cabin and impatiently jabbed my key into the front door. I rattled the key and turned it right and left. I hate locks and keys, and pretty much any kind of metal or container that keeps me from where I want to be. I think it's a leftover from my hippy days. Now that I've almost retired, I've shed the retread hippy look, and returned to my 1960s roots. Finally, through a stroke of luck, I managed to open the door and get into the gallery.

The Diva doesn't let me work in the galley often because I always seem to mess up the cash register, and I've been known to confuse the inventory as well. I do show up a couple of times a week to sign books and teach painting classes; however, I'll do anything in a pinch if someone is sick or can't come in. I really don't mind. I'm sort of a free spirit these days and the gallery is a fun place to work and hang out. Great folks work here, incredible artists hang out here, and even greater people shop here.

Vino followed me around the historic cabin to the front porch and came into the gallery. He knew he was in trouble, so he hung his head and looked pitiful. I relented, as I always do around animals. "Come on out here. I'll clean your face while I drink my coffee." I said as I headed toward the old rocking chair on the front porch. "We've got forty-five minutes before we open."

Vino dutifully followed me and waited patiently while I filled his stainless-steel water bowl. He watched my every move, and when I put his bowl on the porch, I must not have placed it correctly, because he nuzzled it to the right with his nose until he had it in the perfect spot. I shook my head as I watched him drink greedily. When he finished, I was happy to see most of the wine cork had washed off his beard and lay in the bottom of his water bowl. I wondered how much wine he'd consumed. Lots of guests buy the Artisans Gallery's famous wine Slushees and leave part of them in the paper cup for Vino. Oftentimes, they'll purchase a bottle of wine, place their glass on the porch or picnic table, and Vino finds and drinks it... to the last drop. I've even seen him turn a bottle on its side and lick the drops off the side. He's also a master at cleaning wine glasses with his tongue until you can't tell if the wine was white or red. He's a mess around wine.

I inspected his mouth and nose. His muzzle was stained pinkish-purple. He obviously preferred the Cabernets, but the truth is he'll drink anything. Lots of times resort guests just give him wine, and there have been times when Vino's clearly been intoxicated. We've had to stop that. Now, we have a sign on the door that says, "Please do not give our dog wine. We know he loves it, but it's bad for him." I wondered if there was a self-help group for dogs with an alcohol problem.

I'd sat down to enjoy the beautiful fall morning with my now slightly cold coffee when Officer Screech roared into the parking lot. I rolled my eyes and wondered what brought him outside so early on a fall morning. Screech flew out of his car before the police cruiser had even cut off.

"Miss Lily, Miss Lily, sumthin's happened," he hollered, his round face flushed with excitement, his brown eyes bright with anticipation and adventure. Even his cowlick stood higher on his head.

"Mornin', Screech," I said calmly as I stroked Vino's neck. I noticed what appeared to be a mustard stain on his shirt and two missing buttons from his Massanutten Police uniform which allowed his stomach to poke out. I'd heard Screech liked the new hot dog and marshmallow place up at the top of the mountain. I forget the name of it, but it used to be a five-star restaurant named Fairways. The Diva and I would go there after a long day of art sales and have their French onion soup, and of course, a good glass of wine. I have no desire to journey up there for a hot dog and toasted marshmallows.

Screech was so animated that he was unable to speak. His eyes looked like they belonged to a wild man. “What’s up, Screech? You look excited.”

“Is Miss LauraLea here? Is the Diva here?” His voice was eager, his brown eyes poppin’ out of his head as he tried to peer through the window in the cabin.

“Nope, just me.” For some reason, Screech thought he always had to talk to LauraLea when any of us could help. “Check it out. This is what you get,” I said as I pointed at myself. “Now, just spit out what has your knickers in a jam,” I directed him.

Screech clearly considered me second fiddle even though I’d been LauraLea’s partner when we opened the gallery four years ago. Whether he knew it or not, I still had measurable influence.

He stared at me as though he was afraid to open his mouth.

I tossed my head impatiently, stood, and walked to the door. “Okay, whatever. I’ve gotta open this place. It’s almost eleven,” I said as I sipped my now very cold cup of coffee and ruffled Vino’s fur. “If you have something to say, you’d better say it because I’m just about out of time.” I stared at the deputy.

Screech looked uncertain and he raised his hand to push down his cowlick, a nervous habit I’d noticed he had when he was anxious. “Well, I don’t know...” he hesitated. “But, I guess you'll do.” He hesitated again and began, “Well, we had this tip... there's a body down the hill and...” Screech covered his mouth and mumbled. “I'd better wait for Miss LauraLea.”

I'd had enough. I stood up, grabbed my coffee, and entered the gallery to cut on the seventy-five lamps that illuminated the impressive collection of wall art, antiques, handcrafted wood, jewelry, and everything else you'd find in a fine art gallery plus a wine Slushee machine.

Screech followed me into the cabin and in a loud whisper said, “Miss Lily, we got a body, a DEAD body, and it's in your backyard... right down there,” the excited policeman announced as he pointed out the window. “Wanna go with me to see it?”

I stopped in my tracks, turned around, and looked at the deputy. “What did you say?”

“I said we have a DEAD body. Right down there,” he said loudly as he pointed to the woods behind the cabin. “ Screech was so excited he practically jumped for joy.

I felt my heartbeat pick up. Could there really be a body? A dead one? Massanutten's a five-star, four-season resort that includes a relatively sedate community called Massanutten Village located inside the resort. I don't think we'd ever had a murder at the resort or in the Massanutten community.

“Well, you wanna go see it?” Screech's homely face was bright with the thrill of the moment. “The medical examiner will be here soon. I think she's half-way here from Roanoke,” Screech informed me, swollen and puffed up by his self-importance.

I shrugged my shoulders. “Sure, let’s go,” I said as I let Vino into the gallery and closed the door. If there was a crime scene, I sure didn’t want Vino messing it up. He’d probably go down there, spit cork all over the dead person, and screw up everything.

Screech and I walked around the back of the gallery where I saw a couple of wine corks I hadn’t picked up. We walked about a hundred yards down the Arboretum Trail. Shortly after that, we reached the collection of blue stone rock next the end of the trail, a stone’s throw from the Rockingham Spring house.

Screech was so excited he that nearly skipped through the woods. “Lookie over here,” he said excitedly. “Lookie, just look  Miss Lily,” he bellowed as he waved me forward.

I walked toward him, but he held his hand up for me to stop.

“Halt. Stop. Stop right now, Miss Lily. You can’t come no further. This is a crime scene,” Screech informed me as he held up his hand.

I shook my head. “I can’t see anything, Screech. Why’d you bring me down here?” I asked, a little irritated. “I’ve gotta open the gallery,” I checked my watch.

Screech pulled a roll of crime scene tape from his jacket pocket. He pulled off a yard or so and tossed it to me. “Here, walk where I tell you and we’ll mark the scene. I’m the first cop here and it’s my job.” His voice was inflated with self-importance.

I grabbed the yellow tape and paraded in a circle, walking over damp leaves, moss, and sharp rocks. I followed Screech’s commands to a “T.” I spotted two deer watching us with interest, their noses wrinkling and their ears wiggling in the morning sunlight. Then I saw the body.

I'm sure my quick intake of breath and the small sound that escaped from my mouth scared the deer away. I could see the body about forty feet away. It lay by the small pond near some rocks. There were two candles on either side of the victim's head. I knew exactly who it was. *I knew the dead person.* I recognized her coat. Plus, I saw the plastic bag next to her. It was an Artisans Gallery bag, imprinted with our logo. My heart did a flip-flop. Holy crap! It couldn't be. But... I was sure it was.

"Oh, my goodness, Screech! I know who that is," I said as I struggled to control my breath and the timbre of my voice. "At least I think I do," I said in a quieter, hopefully subdued voice."

Screech nodded as he stood next to me. "Somehow, I thought you would, Miss Lily. The dead lady is someone who's been in your gallery."

"In *the* gallery; not *my* gallery," I corrected him. "But yeah, she comes in there all the time and complains about everything we have. She returns most of what she buys." I heard aggravation in my voice. "She was not particularly nice, but I guess we shouldn't speak ill of the dead." I was, if nothing else, a Southern lady, and remembered my manners. I'd been taught many years ago not to speak ill of the dead by my grandmother and my mother. I was still not sure what this Southern mannerism was about. It's not like we have a vote on who gets to heaven. I'm inclined to call things like I see them, especially now.

Screech's not-too-smart eyes bored into mine. I looked back at him. "I'd advise you to not say anything else," he suggested. "I can use it against you, you know." Screech was bloated with importance. "If I feel like it," he said with a wicked grin.

I wanted to flip him off but instead continued to study the body from a distance. "Can I look more closely at the body, Screech? Do you know how she died?"

Screech nodded, "Yep. I think so. Even more importantly, I know the murder weapon," he said with a sly smile. "I know exactly what killed her."

"Can I go closer?" I asked, not sure if I really wanted to.

Screech shook his head. "Nope, not until Dr. Zimbro gets here. She'll be here soon, maybe 'bout a half an hour. She may let you look."

I nodded. I admired Dr. Kenzie Zimbro, our local medical examiner. Kenzie was my friend and an honorary "Artzy Chick." Kenzie lived on the mountain and was a great customer at the gallery. She'd taken every art class we offered, and she helped me all the time with forensic details in my crime novels and medical thrillers.

I gave Screech a dirty look. I supposed he was doing his job, but I wondered why he'd dragged me down here in the first place. I guess to help him unroll the crime tape. Then I wondered why the Massanutten Chief of Police had trusted him with an entire murder scene. Somebody must be out sick, or they must be setting up speed traps on the mountain for the locals.

I shrugged my shoulders and flipped my hair back. "Okay, I've gotta go then. I need to open the gallery. I'm sure there's a dozen people on the porch waiting to get in." I turned to leave.

Screech was panicked. "No, no, please Miss Lily. Don't go. Can't you stay with me for fifteen minutes or so until Dr. Z gets here?" He asked, a hint of fear in his voice. "I don't wanna stay here alone." His brown eyes darted around as he peered through the woods. He pleaded with me, and his arms were outstretched.

I shook my head. Was Screech afraid of the dead person? "No. I've got to go. Call another one of Massanutten's finest," I suggested. "I'm a writer and artist. I don't have any real background in crime scenes," I said although that wasn't really true. I'd written more crime scenes than most police have investigated. I'd worked with a lot of law enforcement officers over the years. That's how I knew some of the Massanutten police were a bit sketchy, and trust me, that's the nicest word I can come up with for them.

Screech's shoulders sagged. "There's no one. They've all gone to Richmond for some dumb weapons class. I'm alone," he admitted as he pleaded. "I need you to stay... be my witness, so I don't get blamed for doing anything wrong," he confided to me. "Please, Miss Lily. This is my first murder."

I shook my head. What the devil was I getting myself into? Number one, I knew the victim; she'd shopped at the gallery last night. Number two, the victim had bats in her belfry, and she hated the gallery. And number three, I had a feeling she had one of my crime novels in that Artisans' Gallery bag. It was possible that the Diva and I were the last two people to see her alive. A dead lady who was a nut case and detested LauraLea and me. This was, for sure, a no win for me.

"Please, Miss Lily." Screech begged me.

Of course, the dead lady disliked most everyone on the mountain. She didn't like the gallery either. Nothing about this was good for me, or LauraLea, for that matter, but I was a softie and let my kindness get in the way of my brainpower.

"Okay, Screech," I consented. "I'll stay for a little while, but I gotta go up to the gallery and get my phone. I've gotta call the Diva or Diane to cover for me. We'll be swamped in thirty minutes," I said as I checked my watch.

Screech gave me a grateful look and, for a moment, I forgot how irritating he was. "Thank you, Miss Lily," he said with a relieved sigh.

I walked back toward the galley and caught a glimpse of red on the ground. I walked off the trail and saw it was a book of matches. I carefully picked it up, touching only the edges. The matches were from the Lonesome Pine Bar in Shenandoah. I'd heard of the place but had never been there. I wished I had a plastic bag. I continued to look for clues on my way back to the gallery, but nothing else caught my eye. "Screech," I yelled. "I'm gonna close the Arboretum Trail. The last thing you need is a bunch of resort guests traipsing around down here."

"Good idea, Miss Lily. That's a really good idea," he said. "Go for it."

"Okay," I said cheerfully. I knew he would never have thought of it.

## Chapter 2

Realization set in and my heart was in my throat by the time I got back to the gallery. A murder. A dead lady I knew... and didn't like. This was the stuff that books were made of. I went inside, found a black magic marker and a piece of cardboard and wrote an ARBORETUM TRAIL CLOSED TODAY sign. I took it outside and stapled it to the Arboretum Trail sign. I knew the last thing Kenzie Z wanted was to have her crime scene trampled by a bunch of Massanutten locals and tourists hoping to glimpse a bear along the way.

I returned to the gallery, grabbed my cell phone, and dialed LauraLea's cell. She answered with her normal smart aleck salutation, "What the heck do you want?"

"You need to get in here. We've got some trouble." I hope my voice didn't sound as frantic as I felt.

The Diva was out of breath when she answered the phone. I supposed she was at the gym or something like that... or maybe she'd just styled her hair and waved her arms around her head. One never knew with LauraLea.

"What's up, Lily? Are you late getting to the gallery?" She asked sarcastically. If the truth were known, neither of us could get anywhere early.

"Yeah, I'm here, and you need to get here as soon as you can," I said impatiently.

"No way," LauraLea said. "I'm coming in at two to do wine tastings and pour the wine. Not one minute sooner."

"Nope," I insisted. "*Now.* We've got a dead body in the backyard."

"What? What did you say? Are you kidding me? No way." LauraLea laughed. She didn't believe me.

"I'm not kidding. I'm serious as a train wreck. I've seen her, and Screech is down there guarding the corpse."

I could only imagine the look on the Diva's face and her magnificent eye roll. "Screech, they sent Screech to investigate a murder? Are they nuts?" LauraLea's voice was condescending. She hesitated and continued, "No never mind, you don't have to answer that," she said with short laugh.

"Seriously, LauraLea, you need to get in here. I'm serious. We know the dead lady and she's not one of our favorite people."

LauraLea was silent for a second. "Oh? Who is it?" She asked in a quiet voice.

"It's Sally Sue Baxter." I whispered, but I'm not sure why. "At least it looked like her. Same coat. Screech wouldn't let me get too close."

LauraLea said one of those words I usually don't write in my books. She let out a long whistle. "Sally Sue Baxter? Of all people. And she's been murdered in our backyard?" I could only imagine the look on LauraLea's face.

"Yep," I confirmed. "I saw her body down by the pond, just off the Arboretum Trail." I waited for LauraLea to comprehend and then added, "and there are two of our soy lotion candles and an Artisans Gallery bag right next to her."

LauraLea was silent, something that generally never happens. I waited about thirty or forty seconds, which seemed like an eternity and then repeated myself. “We have a dead body on the Arboretum Trail, and it’s someone we know.”

LauraLea recovered enough to say, “A dead body? Sally Sue, right? We had nothing to do with it, at least nothing I know of.” Her voice was hushed with a touch of frantic.

I shook my head. “No kidding. But, it’s Sally Sue Baxter, and she *was* our last customer last night. It’s possible that you and I were the last people to see her alive. At least that’s what Screech said to me.”

“Screech, oh my gosh! Who else is down there? I can’t believe they sent Screech out to investigate a murder by himself.” LauraLea said in dumb-founded voice.

I laughed. “Yeah, well they did. He’s the only cop on the mountain. Apparently, all the rest of them are in weapons class in Richmond today,” I said with the least amount of sarcasm I could.

LauraLea was silent for a moment and finally said, “And you’re sure it’s Sally Sue Baxter? Everyone knows she hated us.”

My heart raced a bit as I considered LauraLea’s implication. “Yeah, but she didn’t just hate us. She hated almost everyone. I heard they might throw her out of the Women’s Club.”

LauraLea sighed deeply and said, “They’ve been sayin’ that for years. I’m sorry the old girl’s dead, but she’s been a thorn in our side and a boil on our butt – and most everyone else’s on the mountain – forever.”

"No argument here," I said. "But, you need to get in here. Screech has already said, in so many words, that we're suspects. She has an Artisans Gallery bag next to her body, and somebody, I suppose the killer, lit a candle, maybe two candles, close to her head." I paused for a response, but there wasn't one. "The candle burned all night in the woods... at least, that's what Screech told me."

"What?" LauraLea asked as I heard her drop another four-letter unmentionable word. "Why did the killer light a candle? That's weird."

"No argument here," I agreed. "Maybe it was a scent that keeps the animals away," I suggested.

The Diva thought for a minute and said, "Perhaps. That's possible. Okay, let me get a shower and dressed, and I'll be right in."

"All right, but hurry up, cars are pulling up already, and everyone wants to know why the Arboretum Trail is closed," I said desperately as I watched the cars line up and fight for parking places.

"Okay, can you call Denease? This is perfect chaos management for her. She's the calmest staff member we have." LauraLea rolled her eyes.

"LauraLea, stop that! Denease's a great Christian girl. But it is a great idea," I agreed. "If all else fails, she can sing a little gospel music to them. I'll get her on the horn, but you need to hurry and get your butt in here."

I picked up my phone and called Denease Wyatt. Denease is one of our star salespeople. She is truly a lady, very soft-spoken, dresses like a million dollars, and the shoppers love her. She always looks like a fashion statement in her cute little skirts, cowgirl boots, and statement necklaces. In truth, Denease is a Godsend to Artisans Gallery. She's from Nashville and best of all... she has great stories that entertain our guests for hours. Her cousin was the great Patsy Cline who hailed from up the road from us. In truth, we live in country music heaven. The Statler Brothers came from right down the road in Staunton. Still, that didn't change the fact that we had a murder in the backyard.

Read more on Amazon!

## Also by Judith Lucci

### Alexandra Destephano Novels

*Chaos at Crescent City Medical Center*
*The Imposter*
*Viral Intent: Terror in New Orleans*
*Toxic New Year: The Day That Wouldn't End*
*Evil: Finding St. Germaine*
*Run for Your Life*

### Michaela McPherson Novels

*The Case of Dr. Dude*
*The Case of the Dead Dowager*
*The Case of the Man Overboard*
*The Case of the Very Dead Lawyer*

### Artzy Chicks Mysteries

*The Most Wonderful Crime of the Year*
*Gawd Almighty and the Corn*
*The Jewel Heist*
*Death on the Slopes*

### Other Great Books

*Beach Traffic: The Ocean Can be Deadly!*
*Ebola: What You Must Know to Stay Safe*
*Meandering, Musing & Inspiration for the Soul*